FIRE AND BRIMSTONE

Other books by S. J. Stewart:

Vengeance Canyon
Shadow of the Gallows
Outlaw's Quarry
Beyond the Verde River
Blood Debt

FIRE AND BRIMSTONE

•

S. J. Stewart

AVALON BOOKS
NEW YORK

Published by Thomas Bouregy & Co., Inc.
160 Madison Avenue, New York, NY 10016

Library of Congress Cataloging-in-Publication Data

Stewart, S. J.
  Fire and brimstone / S.J. Stewart.
        p.   cm.
     ISBN 978-0-8034-9851-8 (acid-free paper)
     I. Title.

     PS3569.T473F57 2007
     813'.54—dc22

                                        2007011971

PRINTED IN THE UNITED STATES OF AMERICA
ON ACID-FREE PAPER
BY HADDON CRAFTSMEN, BLOOMSBURG, PENNSYLVANIA

To my sister-in-law and brother-in-law,
Susan and John Edmiston.

Chapter One

Shad Wakefield topped a rise overlooking Judge Harley Madison's Lazy M ranch and reined up. As he watched from his vantage point, he had an uneasy feeling that something was wrong. Everything was quiet. Too quiet. There wasn't a soul in sight, and the place looked downright deserted. At this time of day smoke should be rising from the cookshack, and there ought to be activity around the corral and the barn.

"Something's wrong, fella," he said to Squire, his dun gelding. "I expect we'd better go down and have a look around."

He approached the house with caution, not knowing what to expect. The Judge was aware he was coming today to discuss the business of his own ranch, the M Bar W, in which the Judge was an equal partner.

When still a boy, Shad lost his lawman father to an

1

outlaw's bullet. It was the Judge who'd stepped in to become his guardian. He'd seen to his upbringing and his education. Now twenty-five, Shad still regarded the older man as a foster father. He and the Judge bore no resemblance to each other, nor should they. Shad was taller, reaching a full six feet, and while the Judge's belly had grown paunchy, his own remained lean and well-muscled from hard work. Most noticeable of all, their faces were different. Shad's features were angular, the Judge's soft and round.

A few feet from the house he dismounted and paused to listen. Nothing. He approached the front door. His knock was greeted by silence. He gave a push. The door swung open, and the odor of death came rushing out, coupled with the faint, sulphurous smell of gunpowder. He stepped inside, dreading what he would find. At one end of the room the Judge lay sprawled on the floor in a puddle of blood.

His insides knotted in anger as he knelt beside the body. The Judge had been shot twice in the chest. It was murder, plain and simple. The man had been in his own home, unarmed. Shad started to his feet when a shadow fell across him. Light from the doorway was blocked.

"Hold it right there, you no-good coyote!" came the voice of Ponder, one of the Judge's hired hands.

"It's me, Shad Wakefield," he said. "Don't shoot. I found the Judge like this, and I want to know what happened."

"I ain't taking nobody's word for nothin'. You turn around real slow so I can see your face. And keep your hand away from that gun, or I'll shoot you so full of lead, they'll need extra help to carry you to your grave."

The grizzled old man sounded half crazy. Shad did as he was told.

It wasn't until Ponder got a good look at his face that he lowered the hogleg he was holding. "Sorry, Mr. Wakefield," he apologized. "But I had to make sure that you wasn't the no-account that hit me from behind."

One glance told him that Stu Ponder was in bad shape. He looked worse than a fellow who'd spent a long night drinking bad rotgut. One side of his head was covered in clotted blood, and a big bruise decorated his badly swollen cheek.

Shad stepped away from the body so that the old cowboy could get a look at it. Ponder's knees buckled, and he dropped into a squat. Resting his injured head in his hands, he rocked back and forth on his heels.

"It must've been Barney Kershaw that done it," he said. "That no-account weasel swore he was going to kill the boss for sending him to prison."

Shad clenched his hands to control the rage that threatened to overcome him. Kershaw was a drunken cowhand who'd shot up a saloon and wounded a couple of innocent bystanders. He had a short fuse that grew shorter under the influence of whiskey. By heaven, he was going to pay.

"Was it Kershaw who hit you?" he asked. "Did you see him?"

The old man shook his head, then groaned from the pain the motion caused. "Nope. How could I? He sneaked up behind me to do his dirty work. But lots of people heard him threaten to kill the Judge."

Ponder was right about that. Shad had been working up north with Luke Crane's outfit at the time. But he'd heard the story secondhand from Moses Gault.

According to Moses, "That sorry excuse of a man stood up and called the Judge an old windbag. Why, he even told him he was going to come back and fill him full of holes when he got loose from prison."

But it was strange that Kershaw had taken so long to get even. He'd been out of prison for almost a year and was living quietly in Trinidad. To all appearances he was a law-abiding citizen. In fact, it was the Judge who'd gotten him a job as a swamper at one of the saloons. He said as much to Ponder.

"Ain't you heard, Mr. Wakefield? Revenge tastes a lot better when it's served cold."

The old man had a point.

"I'm going to have a look around outside," he said. "You staying?"

Ponder grabbed hold of a nearby chair and hauled himself up. "Nope. I'm going with you. I can't do nothing for him here."

Outside, Shad spotted fresh tracks beside Ponder's. If Kershaw had made them, he'd gone to the house as soon as he made sure the old man was out of the way. The Judge had been alone and unarmed when he opened the door to his killer.

"Where did everybody go?" asked Shad. "Why are you the only one left?"

Ponder gave him a look of disgust. "They all took off yesterday. Said they had a better offer to work someplace else. A lot better offer."

"I see."

It appeared that the Judge had been set up. But the men who rode for the Lazy M had shown an appalling lack of loyalty.

"Who was it doing the offering?" he asked.

Ponder shrugged. "Don't know. Didn't make one to me. Not that I'd have taken 'im up on it. The Judge has been good to me, and I've been with him for too many years to take off like the rest of 'em did."

"What did the Judge have to say about it?"

"Just that it's a free country and loyalty was in right poor supply."

At the barn, Shad squatted on his haunches and studied the ground. It had recently been disturbed. It was clear that the killer had approached on horseback, and he'd brought no spare. Yet the tracks of two horses led off to the south.

"One of the Judge's horses is missing," he said. "We'd better have a look."

A quick check of the corral told the story. The Judge's prize California sorrel was gone. He'd paid a fortune for it and named it McBeth. Kershaw had good taste in horseflesh.

"He's headed for New Mexico," said Shad. "I'd bet money on it."

"You going down there after him?" asked Ponder.

"Yep. And all the way to purgatory if necessary."

Ponder fished cigarette makings from a pocket in his vest. His hands shook as he sprinkled tobacco into the thin paper.

"The Judge was a mighty good man," he said. "And I know he done a lot for you after your pa died."

"Yes, he did. He sent me to school in St. Louis. Wanted me to become a lawyer."

"Well, you did, didn't you?"

Shad nodded. "But the law hasn't got much to do with ranching, does it?"

"Maybe not, but it's always good to have another line of work to fall back on."

Shad almost smiled, for those were the exact words the Judge had used on him—more than once. "Maybe I'd better clean and bandage your noggin," he said.

Ponder followed him to the bunkhouse, where Shad washed the blood away and cleansed the wound with alcohol. The old man winced but said nothing. Lastly Shad wrapped a clean bandage around his head.

"Obliged," said Ponder. "Reckon I'll have this skull-buster of a headache for awhile."

"Better take it easy," he cautioned. "But if you'll keep an eye on things, I'll ride into Trinidad and report this to the sheriff."

"Count on me," he said. "But ain't you going south after Kershaw? He's going to get a big lead on you."

"Don't worry. I'll catch him. I promise. But I've got to get the word out about what happened here. Then we're going to have to put the Judge away proper, with lots of folks around, like he would have wanted."

Ponder was clearly skeptical. "I guess you know what's best. At least I hope so. Plenty of folks around here are going to want to see Kershaw hang. The Judge has a whole lot of friends."

Of that, there was no doubt. Harley Madison was a fine man. Better than most. At times he'd even been good to his enemies.

Shad strode back to the house. The old man followed at his heels. There he grabbed the reins of the dun, stepped into the stirrup, and swung his leg over the saddle. "Take care of yourself, Ponder," he said. "I'll be back as soon as I can."

"I'll be here."

He rode toward Trinidad, his spirit heavy. The Judge's murder had been a blow. No doubt it would affect a lot of others the same way.

When at last he reached the outskirts of town, he went directly to Abe Featherstone's place. In St. Louis, where he was educated, they would have called the small adobe house a cottage. It was located behind the Judge's larger, more impressive town house, which Abe looked after when its owner was away at his ranch or on one of his trips to Denver.

Abe must have heard him ride up. He met him at the door. Even though his old friend's hair was streaked with gray, his face appeared youthful. His year of marriage to Larkspur Russell had agreed with him. He looked so content that Shad hated to be the bearer of bad news.

"Come on in, Shadrach," he invited, clearly curious

as to the reason for the unexpected visit during a busy time at the M Bar W. "How's things going at the ranch?"

Without answering, Shad stepped into a neat-looking room with gingham curtains. He was met by the aroma of apple pie. Lark Featherstone had been baking.

"Shad, it's good to see you," greeted his friend's attractive young wife. "I hope you can stay around long enough to have supper with us."

"Hold on a minute, Larkspur," said Abe, reading trouble in Shad's face. "I believe something's wrong,"

"Is it?" she asked, searching for a hint in their visitor's expression.

Shad gripped his hat. "I'm sorry as I can be to have to tell you this," he said, "but somebody shot the Judge today out at the Lazy M. Twice. At close range. Murdered him inside his own house."

Both Featherstones reacted with shock. Abe groped for a chair and sat down, his face ashen.

Lark went and stood beside him. "I can't believe it," she said. "Who'd have done such a thing?"

"Ponder thinks it was Barney Kershaw."

"Did he see it happen?" asked Abe.

"No. The killer hit him on the head and knocked him out for a spell. He didn't see a thing. But he was remembering that threat Kershaw made."

"How did you happen by when you did?" asked his friend.

"The Judge was expecting me to ride over and discuss ranch business with him. M Bar W business. The

Lazy M was entirely his own concern. But when I topped the rise, I saw that the place was too quiet. I suspected something was wrong before I got to the house."

"We need coffee," said Lark. She went to the coffeepot on the stove and poured two cups. One she brought to Shad. The other she took to her husband.

"I've known the Judge for more years than I care to remember," said Abe. "He was a good man."

"I didn't know Harley very long," said Lark, "but I adored him. Abe and I were so pleased when he consented to marry us last year. I simply can't believe that something so terrible has happened."

Abe toyed with his cup, waiting for its contents to cool.

"If I thought Barney Kershaw did the killing," he said, "I'd throw a length of hemp over a tree limb and hang him myself. But it just don't feel right. The Judge has done some fine things for Kershaw. Been a real friend to him. He got him a job at that saloon. Even lent him a little money to get him started. The way Harley told it to me, the Judge didn't much care if it got paid back."

It was rare that anyone used the Judge's Christian name. Mostly he was called the Judge, or Judge Madison.

"Kershaw could have been biding his time, waiting for his chance," said Shad.

"Maybe," said Abe, sounding skeptical. "But, like I said, this just don't feel right to me. It's a hat that don't quite fit Barney Kershaw's head."

"But who else would do such a thing?" asked Lark.

A good question, thought Shad. One he couldn't answer. Instead, he merely shrugged.

"Well, I expect Harley's got more enemies than one," said Abe. "You got any idea where the killer, whoever he is, took off to?"

That was a question he could answer with reasonable certainty. "Yeah. He stole the California sorrel and headed toward New Mexico. I'm on my way to see the sheriff and get the word out about the funeral. As soon as the Judge is put away proper, I'm heading south."

"Well, you've got to eat something first," said Lark. She went to the pie safe and cut them each a piece of fresh-baked apple pie to go with their coffee.

"What can I do to help?" said Abe when they'd cleaned their plates.

"Spread the news. I'm going to talk to Sheriff Baca. Tell him what I know. Then I've got to get back to the ranch. Ponder's there alone with his head banged up. The Judge's hands all quit him yesterday."

"Now, why would they go and do something like that?" Abe wondered aloud.

"According to Ponder, they were offered a lot higher wages someplace else."

His old friend scowled. "Something smells rotten as buzzard carrion. Hiring them men away from the Judge made it easy for the killer to ride in and do his dirty work. Now, how did a fellow as simpleminded and down-and-out as Barney Kershaw manage to pull that off?"

How indeed? Still, Kershaw was at the top of Shad's list.

"Maybe he had a confederate. Someone with a glib tongue who could persuade those men with a lot of promises. Could be that those jobs they were offered don't even exist. Likely they'll come stringing back, trying to get hired on again."

Abe wasn't buying his theory. "I wouldn't be looking forward to Kershaw's necktie party just yet," he said.

His friend's obstinacy annoyed him. "Well, if he didn't do it, he'll probably be working or loafing down at the Scarlet Slipper. I heard he has a room in back. I think I'll check on him, and while I'm there, I'll see if anyone can vouch for his whereabouts this morning."

"A good idea, Shadrach. That'll keep folks from getting riled up at the wrong man."

It was dark by the time Shad walked through the doorway of the Scarlet Slipper Saloon. Already the place was almost full. An oversize painting of a scantily clad woman graced the wall above the mahogany bar. Beneath it stood Hal Jacobs, the mustachioed barkeep.

"What'll you have, Wakefield?" he asked.

"Some information about Kershaw. Has he been around?"

Jacobs looked surprised at his question. "Funny you should ask. He took off early this morning and hasn't been seen since. Guess I'm going to have to clean up and sweep the floor myself."

"Did he say where he was going?"

"Nope. I wouldn't have known he was gone if one of the boys hadn't mentioned he'd seen him leave in a big hurry."

Shad clenched his jaw. So much for Abe's theory of Kershaw's innocence.

"Look, Jacobs, let the sheriff know if he shows up, will you?"

"Sure. What's this all about?"

"Somebody went to the Judge's ranch this morning and shot him. After those threats Kershaw made in the courtroom, he's a murder suspect."

The barkeep looked stunned. "It's hard to believe the Judge is dead," he said. "I'll be sure to tell Barney to have a talk with Baca when he gets back."

"Appreciate it," said Shad. He left the saloon and headed for the jail.

The sheriff looked up when he entered. Baca was still in his early thirties. He was of sturdy build and Mexican ancestry. It was said he was related to one of the early trading families that had founded Trinidad and grown rich on the Santa Fe commerce. So far Baca had been a good lawman, despite the fact he was short on help. He listened intently to Shad's account of the Judge's death.

"I am truly sorry to hear this," he said. "My condolences."

"Thanks. He was a fine man."

"On the surface it appears that Barney Kershaw made good on his threats," Baca mused aloud.

"Yes. I'm going after him right after the burying tomorrow."

"I regret that I don't have the manpower to go myself. But if he's in New Mexico Territory, I'd have no jurisdiction anyway."

"Don't worry about it. This is something I have to do on my own."

Baca nodded. "I understand. The Judge was like a father to you. In your place I'd do the same thing."

They shook hands. Then Shad went outside, into the darkness. On the boardwalk he ran into Abe.

"Word is being spread about the Judge's funeral tomorrow. Me and Lark will be out there first thing in the morning. You going back there now?"

"Yes. I don't want to leave Ponder alone any longer than I have to."

"Then I'll see you early tomorrow."

Shad left Trinidad and rode Squire across the broad expanse of moonlit plain. The solitude was welcome, and memories of his childhood sifted through his mind. But he would find no real solace until his guardian's murderer was caught and made to pay for what he'd done.

True to his word, Abe and his wife arrived early the next morning, having set out before daylight. They were followed by a good many others from Trinidad and the surrounding area. People arrived in buggies, in buckboards and on horseback. Shad's foreman, Dan

McNary, stopped by on his way to town and was shocked to learn of the shooting. He turned right around and rode back to tell the men at the M Bar W.

The Judge's body was prepared, dressed in his best Sunday suit, and placed in a linen-lined pine box Abe had brought out from town.

Finally the service began. A crowd of mourners was gathered on the slope where the grave had been freshly dug. Shad knew that the Judge, a man who loved and needed people, would have been pleased at the turnout. Especially since he liked nothing better than being the center of attention. Harley Madison himself had presided over many such send-offs. His eulogies had been described as eloquent. Shad agreed. The man had a way with words. For the Judge's own farewell, Abe had rounded up a Methodist circuit preacher. He was young and green, and eloquence wasn't one of his attributes, but he made up for it with fervor and sincerity. Molly Perkins concluded the service with a hymn.

Before the funeral Shad talked with several of the Judge's friends. There was a strong undercurrent of anger running beneath their grief. Prevailing opinion condemned Barney Kershaw. The fact that he'd taken off without notice and hadn't returned to his job was causing the doubters to join the believers.

While the women were laying out food for the gathering on makeshift tables, Shad went inside the house and changed his clothes. He stashed his broadcloth suit in the Judge's armoire. Then he slipped out the back door and made his way to the corral, where he saddled and bridled the dun. His saddlebags were already packed, and it took only a moment to fasten his bedroll behind the cantle. From the Judge's stable he borrowed a *grullo* that he knew to have a lot of staying power. It would make a good spare. Lastly, he slid his new Henry rifle into the saddle scabbard and mounted up. His backside had barely touched leather when he spotted Abe sprinting toward him.

"Wait up, Shadrach! You're not leaving without me." He was leading the black with a white blaze that he favored, along with a blood bay that belonged to his wife. He, too, had traded his suit and string tie for trail clothes. Strapped to his hip was one of Mr. Colt's finest products.

"You're not going alone, Shadrach. I owe the Judge more than I can ever repay, and when you catch up with Kershaw, I intend to be there."

It was useless to argue with the older man. He was too stubborn.

"Have you talked this over with Lark?" he asked.

"Yes. She's fine with it. She knows what I have to do."

Ponder's bashed and grizzled head appeared from around a corner of the barn. "I see you fellas are heading out. If I didn't feel like I'd been kicked by an ornery mule, I'd saddle up and go with you."

"Don't you worry none, Stu," said Abe. "We'll get the job done. Besides, we need you to stay here and take care of the place 'til we get back."

Ponder's expression brightened. "I'll sure do 'er," he said.

When they rode out, they weren't able to get away without notice. The Judge's friends and neighbors abandoned their potluck meal in order to see them off. Shad glanced back and saw Lark standing alone to one side. She waved.

"Abe, I think your wife wants you to look back."

His friend turned and waved to his bride of almost a year.

"I hate to leave her," he said. "But I know she'll be fine."

They turned the horses in the direction of Raton Pass, the passageway into New Mexico Territory.

Two nights later they were camped on the south side of the pass. They'd left the mountainous trail and were on the high plains. The Sangre de Cristo Mountains lay to the far west. The old volcano called Capulin rose skyward in the east.

They'd made inquiries of travelers on the trail. Kershaw had been seen, and they were a little more than a day's ride behind him.

Cocooned in his bedroll that night, Shad recalled the trip he and Abe had made to New Mexico a year earlier. They'd been on a mission to find Toby Granger, the runaway son of a dying ranch hand. It was on that journey that Abe had met Lark. It was one of the few good things that had happened.

Unable to sleep, Shad started counting stars. They reminded him of sparks from a campfire. Overhead, the moon was a milky opal on black velvet.

"Shadrach," said Abe from close by, "were you as surprised as me to see Jed Hatten at the Judge's send-off?"

"Guess I was too busy to pay much attention."

"It just seemed odd, that's all."

The scruffy-looking rancher who'd claimed a piece of land north of the Judge's place must have kept his distance. At least he hadn't come forward to shake hands and offer condolences as the others had.

"I reckon it is odd," Shad agreed, "since he and the Judge didn't get along."

"I'd be willing to bet he's up to something, and I wish I knew what it was. Harley told me the man lives like a pig and acts worse."

"I guess the Judge also told you they had an argument. They exchanged some pretty harsh words, from what I heard. Hatten wanted the Judge to sell him his ranch. Didn't want to pay much for it, either. The Judge ordered Hatten off the place. Told him to stay off."

"The fellow's a bully," said Abe. "I don't think much of his nephew, either. Avery, I believe his name is."

"Maybe Hatten was nosing around to see if the Judge was really dead. Might have been trying to find out who owns the place now."

"Have you been wondering about that too, Shadrach?"

Truth to tell, things had happened so fast since he found the body that it never occurred to him. It was a good question.

"Only now that we've started talking about it," he

replied. "He was pretty much alone in the world when it came to relatives."

So far as Shad was aware, the Judge had been as alone as he was. As for his legacy, it was well known that Harley Madison was one of the richest men in Las Animas County. Besides the house and property in town, and the ranch where he lived, he was half owner of Shad's M Bar W. He owned a lot of cattle and horses, and he'd made a small fortune in commerce as well.

"I'm wondering if Hatten might be in cahoots with Kershaw," he said as an afterthought.

"Now, that would be a pair," said Abe. "Different as chalk and cheese, as my British cousin used to say. No. I can't see the two of them partnering. I can't see Kershaw working for Hatten, either.

Shad felt a stab of irritation. "You're still not convinced that Kershaw is the killer, are you?"

"Nope. I'll admit it doesn't look good for him, but I still don't think he did it."

Abe was stubborn. If he liked a man, he was loyal to the last, even if that loyalty was misplaced.

"How do you explain the fact that he took out of the Scarlet Slipper like a scalded cat and never came back?"

"I can't," Abe admitted. "But I expect I'm on the trail of the one fellow who can."

What's more, they were catching up quickly, which gave Shad a good deal of satisfaction.

In the dim light that comes before dawn, they broke camp and continued southward. The September morning was cold. Whenever Shad exhaled, his breath turned to smoke. He would be glad for the warmth of the sun.

Kershaw's trail had been easy to follow, since the stolen sorrel had a nick on its right front shoe. Their quarry had started with a sizable lead, but they were fast closing the gap. As the morning wore on, a brisk wind blew across the plains. It wiped out many of the tracks, but here and there Shad was able to spot a nicked hoofprint.

"Remember now, we're going to bring Kershaw back alive," said Abe.

This was yet another of several warnings. Clearly Abe feared that in the heat of anger, Shad would act as a self-appointed executioner.

"I'll take him alive if I can. That's all I'll promise."

"Good enough."

The land through which they traveled was familiar. They'd passed this way the year before. Vast clumps of yellow chamiza blanketed the landscape. As far as the eye could see, yucca spikes sprang from the dry soil. Because of rumors of isolated Comanche raids, they stayed alert.

Another day's ride brought them to the trail town of Cimarron, a place they both knew well. He noticed that Schultz's saloon was under new management. According to a sign out front, the establishment was now called the Watering Hole. They tied their horses to the hitch rail and went inside. The paunchy barkeep, Schultz, who'd been involved in a gold robbery, had been replaced by a skinny, long-faced fellow. Shad stood at the bar beside his friend and thought about their previous visit. They'd wanted information then. They wanted it now.

"What'll you gents have?" asked the bartender.

"First, a shot of whiskey," said Abe. "Then I'd like to know if you've seen the man we're looking for." He described Kershaw in detail.

The bartender poured their drinks from a bottle in his stock, his expression thoughtful. "Can't say that I've seen him," he said. "But I can give you the name of a fellow who might have."

"I'd be obliged," said Abe, fishing some silver coins from his pocket and setting them on the bar gently, as if they were made of fragile crystal.

The man across the counter eyed the dollars with interest. They far exceeded the price of the whiskey.

"There's a new fellow over at the livery stable. He was in here bragging about a deal he'd just made. The fellow he made it with might be the one you're looking for."

"What kind of deal?" asked Shad.

"Well, a stranger comes riding in on this California sorrel worth a mint of money. He's leading a horse, hard-ridden and not anything close to the sorrel. But it was still a good horse. Anyway, this fellow wants to trade it for a fresh one. Well, Slats has this brown mare. Got a few years on her. He offers to trade straight across. The stranger didn't like the deal too much, but he acted like he didn't want to stick around long enough to find a better one. So he switches his saddle from the sorrel to the mare and takes off with the sorrel on a lead line. Slats was right pleased with himself."

"Did Slats say which way the traveler went?"

"Said he was headed for the canyon."

"Much obliged," said Abe, watching the barkeep scoop up the coins.

When they left the saloon, they went to the cafe where they'd eaten during their last visit to the town. There they dined on mutton stew and big slabs of freshly baked bread. Shad wondered about the town marshal they'd encountered the year before.

"Do you think Glover still has his job?" Shad asked.

"Man like him?" said Abe. "I'd bet on it. He's not the kind of fellow likes to move around if he can help it." Abe had his spoon halfway to his mouth when the door opened. He paused. "Well, speak of the devil."

Shad turned to see Marshal Glover standing in the doorway, big as life. Other than having put on a few pounds, he looked the same as last time. He caught sight of them and headed for their table.

"Howdy, Marshal," Abe greeted him. "Have a seat."

"Don't mind if I do. I heard you two were back in town."

"News sure gets around fast," said Shad. "We've not been here more'n an hour."

"The way it was told to me, you're looking for somebody."

"That's right," said Shad. "We're after a man named Kershaw. Judge Madison was gunned down at his ranch east of Trinidad. Kershaw once threatened to kill him—said it in front of witnesses. What's more, he stole the Judge's sorrel and made a run for it. We intend to bring him back to stand trial."

"You wearing a badge?"

"Nope. This is personal."

Glover looked thoughtful. "Last I heard, Wakefield, you were going back to your ranch to lead a peaceful life."

Shad grimaced. "Tried it. It didn't work. You see, I owe the Judge. He took me in after my pa was bushwhacked, and he's been a second father to me. The least I can do is catch his killer."

Glover scooted his chair back and stood up. "Then I wish you both good hunting. From what I've been told, the fellow you're after left here and headed for the canyon. He's probably on his way to Taos."

Shad knew that this "chance" meeting with Glover was far from accidental. The marshal kept a close watch on his small domain.

"We appreciate your help," he said. "The barkeep at the Watering Hole pointed us in that direction too. It's where we'll be heading as soon as we're through here."

They finished their meal after Glover had gone. Then they paid their bill and went out to the horses. It wasn't long before they'd left the trail town behind them. A sage-scented wind rippled the grass and chamiza. The days were growing shorter as the path of the sun slanted southward. They had only a few hours left before dark, and Shad intended to make the most of them.

As he and Abe rode toward the canyon, he thought about how the Judge's death might affect his life. His friend had started it with his question the night before.

"Abe," he said, "did it occur to you that we might be partners?"

"We've been pards for a long time, Shadrach. I was pards with your pa."

"That's not what I meant. No doubt the Judge left a will. I was thinking there's a chance he left his estate to his best and oldest friend."

"I see. You're wondering if I might be half owner of your M Bar W."

"That's right."

Abe gave him an odd look. "Shadrach, there's some things you don't know about the Judge. He had secrets."

Secrets? The way Abe said the word made the hair on the back of Shad's neck stand up. "What in blazes do you mean by that?"

Abe hesitated. "Well, I guess it's all right to tell you, with him being gone and all. Anyway, you're going to find it out for yourself soon enough."

Shad's patience was sorely taxed. "Spit it out, man. What are you talking about?"

"What I'm trying to say is the Judge had a family."

"What?"

"Just what I said. He had himself a family."

"Well, I sure never heard of one."

Abe sighed. "It's a long story," he said. "You see, he was married for a time to a young woman up in Denver. They had themselves a daughter. Named her Anne."

Nothing could have shocked him more. The Judge's secret had been well kept.

"Abe, never once did he say anything to me about having a wife or a daughter."

"You know that Harley was a private man in a lot of ways. He didn't want people knowing his business. The only reason he told me was because he needed a guardian for Anne if anything happened to him. After her ma died so young, he hired a family in Denver to take care of her."

Now that Abe mentioned it, Shad recalled the Judge's many trips to Denver and his long stays there.

"What's his daughter like?" he asked.

"To be honest, I've never even seen her. But I reckon you'll meet her when we get back. I expect she'll have arrived by then. You see, I sent her a wire as soon as I found out that her pa had been murdered."

"How old is she?"

He thought for a minute. "She'd be somewhere around eighteen, I expect. A pretty girl, according to her pa. She's of an age to be getting married soon, and since she's an heiress, she'll be attracting suitors like honey attracts flies. It's going to be up to us to see that she don't pick the wrong one."

Shad stared into the distance, ashamed of his feeling of being betrayed. This wasn't about the Judge's estate, which neither he nor Abe would inherit. That didn't matter. He already had more than he'd ever expected. It was the fact that, all these years, the Judge had kept his family a secret from him.

"Don't fret," said Abe, sensing his mood. "Harley had his reasons. You'll understand it better when all of this comes out."

More secrets?

"Maybe," Shad conceded. "But he should have trusted me enough to tell me about his family. I always considered myself to be a part of it."

"Son, there were circumstances that wouldn't permit him to live the way he would have preferred. He had his political career to think of. Everybody knows that it won't be too many years before the Territory becomes a state, and that opens up a whole lot of possibilities for an ambitious politician. Harley's name was being spoken in prominent circles. Frankly, his eye was on the United States Senate. Always has been. Imagine that. Harley Madison being one of the first two senators to represent the brand-new state of Colorado."

Shad was imagining it. His mentor had looked like a senator. He also had the ability to orate like a senator. Not even Cicero could outtalk Harley Madison on a subject that inspired his passion. What he couldn't understand was why his daughter had to be kept a secret. Maybe when he met her, she could tell him herself.

Chapter Two

Kershaw was somewhere in the canyon up ahead. His trail was fresh, and it was plain by the depth of the tracks that he was riding the newly acquired mare and leading the sorrel. Unfortunately, they were fast losing the light and would soon be forced to stop and make camp.

"Kershaw's slowing down," said Abe. "He's not pushing hard like he did at first."

"No doubt he thinks he's in the clear, now that he's made it down here to New Mexico."

"Then he doesn't know you very well, my friend. Fact is, he doesn't know you at all."

But Abe did. Abe was aware of the temptation Shad struggled with. The temptation to avenge the Judge his own way, not leave Kershaw's fate to a jury.

When it grew too dark to go on, they stopped for the

night. There, at the shallow end of the high canyon, a bitter wind blew down from the mountain peaks to the west. Abe built a fire in a sheltered spot and put a pot of coffee on to boil. Their meal consisted of bacon and fry bread, along with a handful of dried peaches.

"I feel better now that I've eaten," said Abe. "I expect you do too."

Shad didn't deny it, but in truth he'd only feel better after they had Kershaw in custody. It didn't help matters that he was troubled about his guardian's secret life. He wanted to know more, but Abe kept deflecting his questions. There was nothing to do but wait until his friend was ready to talk about why the Judge had chosen to hide his family.

"Are you thinking about what might happen when we catch up to Kershaw?" asked Abe once their bedrolls were spread on the ground.

"Yeah, I guess I am," he admitted. "A fellow who knows he's facing a rope is as dangerous as a rattler."

"In spite of the unanswered questions, you still think Kershaw is the killer, don't you?"

Actually reason and the need for vengeance were warring inside Shad. He made a stab at defending his position.

"Kershaw is riding a horse that was stolen from the Judge after Ponder was knocked unconscious. He made a run for it. What else am I to think? What will a jury think, for that matter?"

"It's all very nice and neat, ain't it?"

That was what bothered Shad the most. It was all so

nice and neat. Disloyal hands hired away by someone unknown. The Judge left vulnerable to attack. A newcomer to the north who wanted the Judge's land. A trail left that a kid could follow. A man who'd made a public threat against the Judge but who hadn't followed through in almost a year. Maybe Abe was right. Maybe Kershaw was a scapegoat. At any rate, he probably wasn't in this on his own.

"I agree that we should take him alive, Abe. I've got a lot of questions that only Kershaw can answer."

Later, as he lay awake beneath his blankets, he thought of the consequences of killing a man. No matter the circumstances, or how badly a man needed killing, the deed always came back to haunt. Usually on a lonely night when the wind rattled the door on a remote line shack, or when snow was piled halfway to the eaves, the ghosts would come. He knew. He'd been forced to kill—more than once.

In the light from the dying campfire he could see Abe's face, calm in repose. No doubt he was dreaming about the wife he'd left behind. At times Shad envied his friend's newfound happiness and wished the same for himself. But like his pa had told him long ago, if wishes were horses, all beggars would ride.

He managed to sleep a little, and at first light they moved out. Scrubby *piñons* and junipers gave way to the taller pines and Gambel oaks. The wooded slopes of the canyon rose high above them on either side. The air was pine-scented. Beside them, the Cimarron River played its own kind of music as it rushed eastward toward the Nations.

An hour passed, and then another, as they moved deeper into the high canyon that had been cut by the powerful river over years too many to count. In places the tree-covered slopes gave way to bare-rock cliffs, their faces worn into lines of ribbed corduroy by the forces of nature. Shadow and sunlight played across this canvas of stone, creating an ever-changing work of art. On the narrow trail they followed lay fresh horse droppings, evidence that Kershaw was close by.

"Careful, now," warned Abe. "He could be hiding anywhere."

Shad scanned the slopes, trying to spot any sign of him. The warning came when a horse nickered from cover at their own mounts. He and Abe slid from their saddles. A shot was fired from somewhere up ahead. They dove for cover.

"Get out of here!" Kershaw yelled. "I didn't do nothing. Go away and leave me alone."

"I'll talk to him," Abe whispered. "He knows me better."

Shad was glad to leave it to him.

"Hey, Barney, come on out and talk to us. It's me, Abe Featherstone. Me and Shad Wakefield just want to ask you a few questions."

"Don't give me that! I know what you want to do. You want to take me back so they can string me up."

"Now, why do you think that?"

"The friend who gave me this here sorrel told me. Said somebody killed the Judge and they was going to lynch me for the murder. Told me I had to run for it."

"Where'd you get that gun?" said Abe. "I didn't know you carried one."

"From the same friend who gave me the horse. He told me to shoot anybody who tried to take me. I'll do it too."

"Why, Barney," said Abe in his most soothing voice, "I never knowed you to shoot at anybody 'cept when you was drunk."

"Well, I ain't drunk now, and you just heard me shoot. I'm telling you, Featherstone, you ain't taking me back to no lynch mob."

Abe was getting exactly nowhere. Kershaw was too scared to listen to reason.

"Keep him talking," Shad whispered. "I'm going to circle around and get behind him."

Abe nodded and continued. "Tell us about this friend of yours, Barney. Maybe I know him. What's his name?"

"How should I know? He didn't introduce himself, and he had his hat pulled down to hide his face."

While Abe was distracting him with questions, Shad moved up the slope like a ghost. He used scrub and pine for cover as he worked his way up behind Kershaw. When he reached a spot a few feet away, he stopped.

"You don't believe me," shouted the fugitive. "Ain't

nobody going to believe me. Go away! Leave me alone!"

Kershaw lifted the pistol and aimed it at the place where Abe was crouched. Before he could fire off another shot, Shad lunged and grabbed his wrist. Kershaw struggled, but Shad managed to twist the revolver from his grasp.

Abe ran up the slope to them. "Let me have a look at that gun."

It was an old Army Colt. When Abe broke it open, he found only two bullets in the chambers. "Got any more ammunition?" he asked Kershaw.

"No," said Kershaw, ashen-faced and trembling. "All I got is what's in the gun. Guess my friend didn't think to give me any extra."

"Convenient," said Shad, his voice heavy with sarcasm. "I've got a hunch it was two bullets from this gun that killed the Judge. You count the one Kershaw just fired, make allowance for the empty chamber that most men use for safety's sake, and that leaves the two that're here."

"I see what you mean," said Abe. "Our friend here was set up to die."

"What are you talkin' about?" said Kershaw.

"You were given the weapon that killed the Judge," said Shad. "The killer left you three shots. Just enough to provoke us to shoot back. At which time you'd be buzzard bait."

Kershaw's knees buckled, and he sat down.

Abe hunkered down beside him. "Before we go another step, Barney, you need to tell us everything you know about this situation," he said. "We're your only hope."

Shad thought the man was going to blubber, but he managed to pull himself together.

"It all started when a fellow came to the back of the saloon where I work and handed me a note. Well, I don't read too good, so I asked him to tell me what was in it. He said it was urgent. Said I was to meet a man out at Grove's Hollow. That my life depended on it. I was to go right away and not say a word to anybody."

"And you went along with that?" said Abe.

"What else could I do? Well, when I got to Grove's Hollow, sure enough there was a man waiting for me. He had this fine sorrel with him. He told me the Judge had been murdered. Said everyone was going to think I'd done it, and if I didn't run, they'd come and string me up. Well, he gave me the sorrel and handed me the gun for protection."

"What did he look like?"

"I told you, I don't know. His hat was pulled low and shaded his face. Besides, I was so scared that I didn't pay much attention. Nothing about him stood out to be remembered. He had all of his limbs, and no scars were showing. He wasn't short nor tall, and he wore a beard like a lot of other fellows do. It was rusty colored. Strange thing, though. The horse he rode wasn't near as good as the one he handed over to me."

"I can shed some light on that," said Abe. "That sorrel was stolen from the Judge, and it has a nick in one of its shoes. It left a trail that even a child could follow."

"In other words," said Shad, "the killer made you a scapegoat. With you dead, no one would ever look for him."

It was a nasty scheme, but it had almost worked.

Abe went and had a look inside Kershaw's saddlebags. He pulled out two bottles and held them up. "I see you stopped long enough to steal a couple bottles of the finest whiskey."

Kershaw flushed. "I didn't steal nothin'. That was something else the fellow at Grove's Hollow gave me. He said I'd need 'em."

"Looks like the killer wasn't taking any chances," said Abe. "You've got a reputation for wildness when you're drinking." He put the bottles back where he'd found them.

Kershaw looked up with red-rimmed eyes that were sad as a hound dog's. "You can't take me back to Trinidad. They won't believe a word I say."

"You're probably right," Abe agreed. "Folks ofttimes let their feelings get in the way of their common sense. Still, you've got to return with us and tell the sheriff your story. We'll back you up on it."

Shad had an idea. "Surely you can you describe the messenger who came to the saloon with the note?"

"Of course I can," said Kershaw. "He was a young fellow, not any older than you. And he read real well. He was educated for sure, and good-looking too. You know, the kind that the ladies all want to dance with at the socials."

"Go on," Shad urged.

"He had dark hair and dark eyes, and he was taller than me. I noticed that he wore nice boots. There wasn't hardly any signs of wear on 'em at all."

Shad gave Abe a knowing look. Kershaw had just described Avery Hatten, Jed Hatten's nephew. What's more, Jed Hatten had a rusty-colored beard. The stranger at Grove's Hollow must have been the uncle. It appeared the motive for the Judge's murder wasn't revenge but greed. With Kershaw blamed for the murder, Hatten had a clear field with the Judge's heir.

The Hattens were newcomers to the area. Mostly they kept to themselves, except for Avery, who rode into town once or twice a week and went to some of the dances. Jed was a lot less sociable, and he'd earned a reputation for being a fellow you didn't want to cross. But nobody seemed to know where they'd come from or where they'd gotten the money to stock a ranch and pay a bunch of ranch hands.

"Get on your horse," said Abe. "We've got a lot of riding to do."

"I ain't going," said Kershaw, who was on his feet now. "No man with any smarts would put his own head in a noose."

"They're not going to hang you if me and Shad have anything to say about it."

"Well, they might not let you have any say."

Shad was losing patience. "Let me put it this way, Kershaw. You don't have a choice."

The slight, balding man, who'd looked bad before,

looked worse now. It was as if he was picturing himself on the steps of the gallows.

"And don't try to make a break for it either," said Abe. "You do, and you'll miss out on my cooking."

While Abe set about fixing a meal, Shad kept an eye on the skittish prisoner. Trapped and scared as he was, Kershaw still managed to eat his fill of pan bread and bacon.

As soon as they were finished, they packed and mounted up. With Kershaw under Abe's watchful eye, they headed back the way they'd come. When it got dark, they camped again in the canyon.

After they'd eaten and the fire was burning low, Abe fetched a length of rope and stood in front of the prisoner.

"I hate to do this to you, Barney," he said, "but I have to make sure you don't run out on us."

Kershaw backed away. "You going to tie me up?" he said, his voice coming out as a squeak. "You and who else?"

"Now, don't make this difficult, Barney. You know good and well that the first chance you got, you'd sneak off."

Shad stood in the light of the low-burning flames and touched the grip of his revolver. Kershaw saw this deliberate motion, as was intended. The fight went out of him. He remained docile as Abe secured him to a tree and threw a horse blanket over him.

"This should keep you warm," he said. "We ride at dawn."

Shad watched the prisoner settle down to sleep. Then he moved away from the dying fire and made his way to the darkest shadows of the juniper-covered slope. There he bedded down. Above him, through openings among the branches, the low-hanging stars shed their light. The sight was enough to tempt a man to keep looking upward.

As he was drifting off to sleep, a thought occurred to him. If he were in Hatten's place, he wouldn't leave *anything* to chance. He'd have sent one of his men along to keep an eye on things, someone who would hide in the background and follow Kershaw's trail. Someone who could report back that the plan had succeeded. This was a troubling notion. He patted the stock of the rifle that lay beside him. The smooth, hard feel of the wood was comforting.

Before dawn, when there was just enough light to see by, he crawled out of his blankets and slipped away from the camp. In order to spy on them, Hatten's man would have chosen a spot close by. Had Shad been in his place, he would have positioned himself on the opposite slope. He headed that way on foot with both pistol and rifle. It didn't take long to find what he was looking for. Boot prints remained in a patch of soft earth overlooking their camp. The man's horse had been tied to a nearby branch. Gun drawn, Shad looked around. But the spy had pulled out.

"You're up and about early," said Abe when he returned to camp.

"I had a hunch that Hatten sent one of his men to make sure we killed Kershaw. I was right. He was up there, watching us." He pointed to the spot.

Kershaw looked shaken. "See? I told you I didn't have a chance," he said.

"Actually, you've got one, but only one," said Shad. "If you don't come with us and tell the sheriff what happened, your 'friend,' Jed Hatten, will have you killed off as soon as he gets word that you're still alive and able to expose him."

The man's slight body seemed to shrink even more. "I was over there all night, helpless, tied to that tree. If he'd wanted to kill me, he would have. You ain't no protection to me."

"The man didn't have orders from his boss to kill you," said Shad. "It was supposed to look like we were the ones who shot you, either in self-defense or in a frenzy of vengeance. Otherwise, there'd be a lot of questions asked, and Hatten can't stand the scrutiny."

Kershaw looked unconvinced. "You've gotta give me back the gun and some ammunition," he pleaded.

Abe gave him a withering look. "My mama didn't raise no fools. I'm not about to let you get hold of a weapon. Besides, I expect the sheriff will want to have a look at that gun Hatten gave you."

Kershaw wilted. The man was spineless. Shad understood why the Judge had taken pity on him.

They broke camp and rode east toward Cimarron. On the way they crossed the tracks of Hatten's spy. Shad knew they were in a race. They had to get Kershaw to the sheriff before Hatten got word that his scapegoat was still alive.

There was little talk, as each man was kept company by his own thoughts. When they rode into Cimarron, they stopped at the livery stable on the edge of town to feed and water their horses.

"Wait for me here," said Shad. "I want to find Marshal Glover and have a few words with him before we leave."

"We'll be here," said Abe.

Shad made his way down the street to the jail. When he stepped inside the small office, Glover looked up from his work.

"Well, hello again, Wakefield. Have a seat. Did you find your man?"

"Yes," he said, pulling up a chair. "But the trouble is, he's not the Judge's killer."

The marshal's eyebrows went up in surprise. "Do tell. You know this for sure?"

"Yes. He was set up by the killer."

"Got any idea who that might be?"

"We do now."

He told the marshal about the meeting at Grove's Hollow, the gun with three bullets, the stolen sorrel with the nicked shoe, and the bottles of whiskey.

"I should have suspected Jed Hatten all along," said Shad. "He's been feuding with the Judge over his land. But Kershaw had made threats, so everybody figured he was the one. None of us investigated any further."

"Looks like that's the way this Hatten fellow had it planned. But what is it I can do for you, Wakefield?"

"You know about everything that goes on in this town. Did you happen to see a stranger ride through from the direction of the canyon earlier today? He'd be acting like he was in a big hurry to get somewhere else."

Glover nodded. "Matter of fact, I did. He's not too far ahead of you. Maybe three or four hours."

"Can you describe him?"

Glover thought for a minute. "I'd say he's young. Early twenties. Tall. Had a pretty face, too. The kind that my niece and her friends would swoon over. He wore expensive clothes. Not much wear on 'em. He stopped at the cafe long enough to get something to eat. Then he mounted up and hightailed it out of here."

"Obliged for the information. You've just described the killer's nephew. Name's Avery Hatten. He's part of an outfit that moved onto a ranch north of the Judge's place awhile back. Can't say anything good about 'em. Don't know what the folks would say about 'em wherever it was they came from."

"Glad to help anytime I can. Now, you'd better get a move on if you aim to catch up with that fellow."

Back at the stable, Abe could tell by Shad's expression that he'd learned something. "Out with it," he said.

"Avery Hatten was through here. He's got a three- or four-hour lead on us."

"You ain't never going to catch him," said Kershaw. "You might as well give it up."

"Don't be so gloomy," said Abe. "That kind of thinking wears on a man."

Kershaw muttered something under his breath that sounded suspiciously like a curse.

They didn't waste any time leaving Cimarron behind and were soon on the high plains again with the mountains behind them. It was possible to see for a great distance, but there was no sign of Avery.

It wasn't that Shad had any real hope of stopping Hatten's nephew. What they had to do was get Kershaw safely to Sheriff Baca before word got back to the elder Hatten that Kershaw was still alive. Shad suspected that a man as ruthless as Jed Hatten had WANTED dodgers floating around. Maybe that was why he kept so much to himself. It was something Baca needed to check out.

"Look, you know this ain't right," said Kershaw after a time of blessed silence. "Let me go, and I'll head straight for Mexico. You'll never see me around here again."

"Afraid we can't do that," said Shad. "There's a killer to catch, and we need you to tell your story. I promise we won't let you take the blame for a killing you didn't do."

Kershaw wasn't reassured.

"Now that all three of us know it was Hatten who killed the Judge, that no-account can't afford to let any of us live," said Abe.

Shad had reached that conclusion back in the canyon. All it would take to rid Hatten of his problem was three well-placed sniper's bullets. But they didn't have any more choice than Kershaw. They had to take him in.

They weren't more than a day's ride from Trinidad when they stopped beside the Santa Fe commerce trail and made camp. Though it was late in the year and snow threatened to fly in the high places, they had plenty of company on the road. A big wagon train had halted for the night just to the north.

Kershaw was jumpy. Even more so than usual. They were getting close to Trinidad and its townfolk, so Shad figured he had a right to be. As for Abe, he seemed moody and lost in thought. Not only did he have the Hatten bunch to deal with, but when they got back to the Lazy M, he'd have to take care of the Judge's daughter. That is, if she'd arrived. No doubt about it, his friend had a lot of responsibility on his shoulders.

Shortly after daybreak they began the last leg of their journey. It had been ten days since the Judge's murder. They passed the wagon train, quickly leaving the heavy-laden vehicles, yokes of oxen, and short-tempered teamsters behind. When they were beyond Wootton's place, located near the toll road through the pass, Shad spotted his foreman from the M Bar W, Dan McNary, on horseback.

McNary rode up to them at a gallop. "I see you fellows got your man," he said, giving Kershaw a hostile look. "Where'd you find him?"

"Cimarron Canyon," said Shad.

"He ain't the one who done the killing, though," said

Abe. "He was set up by that Hatten bunch. I expect Jed Hatten himself shot the Judge. But his nephew, Avery, was in on it. The rest of 'em too, no doubt."

McNary leaned forward, his face alive with interest. "If this is true, then it explains a lot that's been going on."

"Like what?" asked Shad.

"Look, I think maybe we'd better talk while we ride."

"You're right," said Shad. "I need to get to Trinidad as soon as possible and make a report to Sheriff Baca."

"I wouldn't advise that," said McNary. "Hatten's been setting things up while you were gone. From what I hear, he's got Baca eating out of his hand. What's more, a young woman arrived on the stage, claiming to be the Judge's daughter. The whole town is buzzing. Hatten didn't waste any time taking her out to his place, and, according to witnesses, she was quite willing to accompany him."

Shad was astonished that such a thing could happen. He glanced at Abe, who wore an expression of righteous fury.

"The nerve of that outlaw!" he cried.

McNary nodded in agreement. "Being that you knew the Judge so well, Abe, I guess it's no surprise to you that he had a daughter."

"No. But I figured she'd have sense enough to stay in town at the hotel until I could get back and take her to the ranch. For that matter, she could have stayed with Lark."

"Well, her actions are puzzling, to say the least," said

McNary. "It's hard to imagine any well-bred young woman staying out at that hog wallow Hatten calls home. But that's not all. He's been planting suspicion in people's minds about you and Abe, not to mention everyone else out at the M Bar W. That's why I've been waiting for you. Hatten's been telling it around town that he heard you and Abe hire Kershaw to murder the Judge so you could inherit his property. Abe is supposed to be in on it for half of everything. Hatten told the sheriff that you went after Kershaw to kill him so he couldn't talk."

Now it was Shad's turn to be furious. How could anyone believe such hogwash? But if he'd killed Kershaw like he'd wanted to do, like he was supposed to have done, that's exactly what it would have looked like.

"You've heard quite a lot, McNary," said Abe.

"A fellow who used to work for Hatten quit the other day. He rode up and asked for a job. We needed help, so I hired him.

"He mentioned that he saw the Judge's daughter when she arrived Said she was blond, well-dressed, and pretty, in a hard sort of way. But she was uppity and rude. After Hatten spoke to her, she went to Baca and demanded he send a posse after you. She wants to see you both hang."

So, Hatten had meant to discredit them from the beginning. What better revenge on the Judge than to have his two best friends strung up for his murder?

"They're expecting us to ride into Trinidad," said Shad. "I think we'd better start doing the unexpected."

McNary agreed. "Hatten has men posted on the lookout for you. He can't afford to have you talking to the sheriff."

"Let's go to the Judge's ranch until we can decide on our next move," said Shad.

"I'll ride with you," McNary said.

The men veered off to the east, avoiding Trinidad altogether. It seemed to Shad that the description of the female McNary had passed along was out of keeping with a gently reared young woman who was related to the Judge. Then, too, why would she believe the lies of a rough-looking stranger who was conveniently in town to meet her stage? The Judge's daughter would surely know that he and Abe were the Judge's most loyal friends.

Shad was willing to bet his ranch that the real Anne Madison was somewhere else—and that the woman who'd taken up with Hatten was an imposter.

He was glad McNary was with them. Dan was a good man to have around when there was trouble. Short and stocky, McNary could hold his own with guns, fists, or even with words when called upon. His slight limp didn't hinder him either, since most of his time was spent in the saddle.

Shad hated to think what would have happened if they'd ridden into Trinidad, unaware of Hatten's treachery. He knew how quickly friends could be turned into enemies, neighbors into a mob. It was thanks to McNary that they were on their way to the relative safety of the Judge's ranch.

Chapter Three

Sunlight washed over the vast short-grass plains. A light wind rippled across them. Near a stream bed a stand of cottonwoods was crowned in autumn gold. Still, Shad's mood was dark. Hoodwinked by Hatten, he'd wasted precious days. He was angry, and that anger lay coiled inside him like a deadly snake that could, at any moment, strike out.

"I did a little scouting before I went to meet you," said McNary. "It wasn't just the southern approach to town that Hatten has blocked. He has men posted at all of them. None of us has much chance of getting through to Sheriff Baca with the truth. Like it or not, we're on our own."

"I can't understand it," said Abe. "Why didn't someone stop Hatten from luring Anne away from town? Except for that old Ute woman who's said to work for him as a cook, there's no other female up at his place. Leastwise none that I've heard of. And the shack, by all accounts, is filthy and run-down."

From McNary's description, Shad concluded that it hadn't taken much "luring." Abe, however, was still clinging to the possibility that Hatten's woman was the real Anne Madison. No one could blame him. But Shad was convinced she was a fake. And there was no telling what had happened to the real one.

"According to our new hired hand," said McNary, "the woman appeared eager to go with Hatten. Said she welcomed his protection. May be she and Hatten weren't strangers at all."

Abe looked stricken. McNary was stripping away his last hope. "Well, maybe she's who she says she is, and maybe she's not," he said. "But either way, I'm going up there to bring her back to the Lazy M."

McNary shook his head. "I wouldn't try it if I were you, my friend. You're apt to get shot. That blond woman might even do the job herself. The way that hand told it, she believed Hatten's story about you and Shad hiring Kershaw to kill the Judge so you could grab her inheritance. And she went straight to Baca. Some of the townspeople have already turned against you and want to see you hang alongside Kershaw."

"That does it," said Shad. "That woman was too well rehearsed. There's no way she could have formed an honest opinion and started condemning us the moment she stepped off the stagecoach."

Abe's expression was grim. No doubt he was afraid

for his ward. Hatten and his outfit must have done something with the real Anne Madison to keep her out of the way of her replacement. Whatever it was couldn't be good.

"Most of the people in Trinidad know us too well to believe such lies," said Abe.

McNary disagreed. "Hatten swore that he overheard you and Shad hiring Kershaw to kill the Judge. Said the three of you were behind the privy in back of the saloon when he went out to pay it a visit. Said he went to the sheriff only once Miss Anne Madison was safe under his protection. It appears he was convincing, at least to some."

Shad gripped the reins tightly and uttered a curse under his breath. "Repeat a lie often enough and convincingly enough," he said, "and even the skeptics start accepting it as the truth."

A groan issued from Kershaw, who'd been riding quietly beside them. "I'm a dead man," he said. "But it looks like the rest of you ain't going to come out any better'n me."

"Don't count us out yet," said Shad.

"Easy to say, but I wish I was down in Mexico. It'd sure be better'n here."

Shad thought about the blond woman. "Abe, didn't you tell me that you'd never seen Anne Madison?"

"That's right. But don't worry. I have a surefire way of telling if this girl is the genuine article. A way that would convince everyone. Although not from a distance and not without her cooperation."

Not much help.

"Who were those people she was living with?" said Shad.

"Their name is Bolin. I'll wire them to see what they know about this. Might help us find the real Anne Madison, if this one isn't it."

"If she's still alive," added Kershaw.

Shad caught a glimpse of Abe's pained expression and wished that Kershaw had kept his mouth shut.

"If that woman is working for Hatten," said McNary, "he's using her to get his hands on the Judge's property, sure as shootin'."

"Hatten's been trying to get his hands on the Lazy M for some time now," agreed Shad. "It's a nasty little scheme, and we can't let him get away with it."

He remembered Abe's comment about how Hatten had showed up at the Judge's send-off and how he'd thought his presence was odd. Maybe Hatten had come to gloat. That, and to see if they'd take his bait and ride out on the trail of the scapegoat.

"I looked in on Ponder before riding out to meet you," said McNary. "Toby came with me, and I left him there to help out. I didn't think the old man should be left alone to do everything himself. Still, under the circumstances, we'll need more men."

Toby Granger was the seventeen-year-old son of a ranch hand who'd died the previous fall. Before Nat Granger's death, he'd asked Shad to go down to the gold camps of New Mexico, find his runaway son, and fetch him back. He and Abe had made it in time for

Toby to reconcile with Nat before the end. Since his father's death, Toby had settled down and was shaping up to be a good worker. Shad approved of McNary's leaving him with Ponder. He also agreed they needed to send for more men.

"You don't suppose the Lazy M is being watched?" said Abe.

"Not that I could tell," said McNary. "I think they're concentrating on Trinidad, where they'll expect you to show up to challenge their lies."

Even though the foreman hadn't seen anyone around the Judge's ranch, they still stayed alert as they drew near the house.

The short autumn day was almost gone as they rode up. The Judge's house was bathed in muted light and cloaked in silence. To Shad, the place had an eerie feel about it. When he opened the door and stepped inside, a shudder ran down his spine. He could almost sense the Judge's presence. He lifted a lamp chimney, fumbled for a match, and struck it. When he touched the flame to the wick, light blazed up. He replaced the glass cover and stepped back, watching as the lamp cast shadows on the walls.

He saw that the small rug Lark had thrown over the bloodstained floor was still in place.

"It's getting cool this evening," said Abe, who, along with the others, had joined him.

"Yes. Guess I'd better build a fire to take the chill off."

"While you're doing that, Abe and me will unload the gear," said McNary.

As Shad busied himself with the fire, Kershaw stood off to one side, watching. His face was the picture of hopelessness.

Abe stepped back inside, lowered his saddlebags to the floor, and leaned his rifle against a wall. "I wonder where Ponder and Toby got off to," he said.

"I just spotted them," said McNary, who was a few steps behind him, his arms loaded with gear. "They're on their way."

In a matter of minutes the old man arrived with Toby at his heels.

"Sorry not to be here when you arrived," said Ponder, who was looking a whole lot better than when Shad had last seen him. "We wasn't expecting you back so . . ." He trailed off as his gaze went to Kershaw.

"He didn't do it," said Shad, guessing Ponder's thoughts. "He was framed by Jed Hatten. It was Hatten who killed the Judge, and his nephew was in on it."

"Are you sure about that?" said Ponder, his tone skeptical.

"Yes. He and his nephew, Avery, set Kershaw up so it would look like he was guilty." He repeated the story Kershaw had told him.

"Why would Jed Hatten do something like that?" the old man asked.

Shad guessed that he wasn't around when Hatten and the Judge had argued.

"He wants this ranch, and he wants it bad. He tried to strong-arm the Judge into selling. But you knew Harley Madison. Nothing intimidated him. He ordered

Hatten off his land. Now, with the Judge dead, Hatten's probably got a scheme to get his hands on the place."

"Well," said Ponder, "that sure explains why he was so keen on gettin' that girl away from town and up to his shack. The way that circuit preacher told it when he stopped by, Hatten practically grabbed her off the stage and started filling her head with some wild story. When the preacher told me that the Judge had a daughter, I could scarcely believe it. Anyway, he said that she was demanding your arrest."

It made sense. If the scheme was to work, people would have to think it was the Judge's own daughter discrediting Abe and him, accusing the Judge's best friends of killing him.

"Shad thinks she's an imposter," Abe told Toby.

"You do?" Toby asked.

"That's about the size of it," said Shad.

"No doubt he's right," said Abe. "But I've got to make sure. I've got to go up there and try to fetch her back, whoever she is."

"She won't come," said McNary.

"In any case, I want to look her in the eye and hear what she's got to say."

"Well," said the foreman, "if that's what you're bound to do, you're going to need a show of force."

"Whatever it takes."

"Then wait here until I can fetch some of the boys from the M Bar W."

"That's a good idea," said Shad. "We'll wait for you." He turned to Toby. "If you've had your supper, I want you to ride into Trinidad. I'm pretty sure Hatten's men won't know you. Lie about who you are, if you're stopped. Then go straight to Larkspur Featherstone's house and give her the note I'll send with you. Tell her to pass it along to Sheriff Baca. Have her take him a loaf of bread, a piece of pie, or something, as an excuse to go to the jail. That way no one will suspect."

"I can do that," the boy agreed.

"When you get to my wife's house," said Abe, "tell her I'm back and that I'm fine. The woman tends to worry."

Toby grinned. "I'll tell her you're as ornery as ever."

Shad rummaged through the Judge's desk until he found a piece of paper and a pencil. He scribbled a quick note to the sheriff, telling him what had happened and what he'd learned. When he finished writing, he handed the note to Toby, who slipped it inside his hatband.

"It'll be safe there so long as I don't forget where I put it," he said with a grin.

Shad went outside with the boy and McNary. Toby headed for the corral to fetch his Appaloosa named Banjo. In the meantime Dan mounted up and rode eastward toward the M Bar W. When Toby returned astride the Appaloosa, Shad warned him to be cautious and wished him luck.

"Look, don't worry about me," he said. "I'm not a kid anymore."

He was almost right.

Toby nudged Banjo in the sides and rode off in the

direction of Trinidad. Shad stood there for a time, watching as the boy's shadowy figure grew ever smaller on the moonlit plain. It was then he noticed that the wind had come up. It was out of the north and had a sting to it. He ducked back inside. Abe had a pot of coffee on and was fixing supper.

The house was the Judge's pride and pleasure. It was better built and more luxuriously appointed than most homes in the area. Granted, it might not be up to New York or St. Louis standards, but by those of the plains, it stacked up well, indeed. The Judge had ordered furniture, china, and silverware from St. Louis. Other niceties too. The polished floors were dotted with thick sheepskin rugs. A mahogany rolltop desk stood against one wall. Beside it was a leather-covered chair. The big chair the Judge favored sat near the hearth. Across from it was a rocker. The large bedroom, off to one side, held a carved four-poster and a fancy French armoire. Had she used her head, the woman claiming to be the Judge's daughter could have been staying here in cleanliness and relative luxury, rather than in a hovel with Hatten.

In the dining room, they ate at the long table flanked by carved oak chairs. Kershaw looked uncomfortable at the unaccustomed formality. He glanced nervously at Shad and tried to copy his way of eating.

"Don't worry, Kershaw," Abe assured him. "You're doing just fine."

The saloon swamper turned red in the face. "I don't much eat at a fancy table in front of company," he said. "It takes a mite of getting used to."

When they'd finished the meal and cleaned the dishes, Ponder pulled on his coat and went to the door. "I'm going to go take care of the horses," he said.

Abe grabbed his coat too. "I believe I'll give you a hand. It'll do me good to get some of the kinks worked out of my legs."

That left Shad alone with Kershaw.

"If it's all right with you, Wakefield, I'll throw my blankets in that corner over there. It don't matter much where I sleep."

"Fine with me."

"Is this where you found the Judge?" he asked.

"Yeah. Right over there." He pointed to the spot, now covered by a rug.

Kershaw shuddered. "Do you believe in ghosts and spirits?" he asked.

"I don't know. Maybe. I've never actually seen one, but that doesn't mean they don't exist."

"I seen one once. A fellow died in prison. Stabbed with a pieced-together knife. Crude thing, it was. I was one of half a dozen fellas who came upon his body. Strangest thing. I saw him plain as day, standing over himself and looking like he didn't know what to think. Guess dying was a shock to him. Maybe he wasn't sure he was dead. Anyway, I just stood there. Couldn't say nothing. Then, after a minute, he disappeared into thin air."

"Any of the others see him?"

"Yep. All of 'em did. And one of 'em was a guard.

But we didn't tell nobody. In prison it's smarter to listen than to talk."

While Kershaw finished spreading out his bedding, Shad made himself comfortable in the Judge's big chair. He was almost asleep beside the fire when Ponder and Abe returned, bringing with them a gust of cold wind.

"Temperature's dropping," said Abe. "That fire sure feels good."

The newcomers piled down in their bedrolls and went to sleep. Shad remained in the big chair, quietly watching the flames. It felt to him as if the Judge had only stepped out for a spell and would open the door and come walking in at any time. It was a pleasant but fleeting thought. Jed Hatten had put an end to the Judge's life, and his spirit was gone. Now, very soon, Shad would come face to face with a cold-blooded killer.

The warm room and the crackling fire had a hypnotic effect, and he dozed. His sleep was dreamless as the hours ticked away on the nearby mantel clock. When he opened his eyes, Abe was fixing breakfast.

"Day's half over, Shadrach. 'Bout time you woke up."

Shad unfolded himself from the chair and stretched muscles that ached from inactivity. The others had eaten and were outside preparing to leave.

"McNary isn't back yet, is he?"

"Nope. But he ought to be getting here before long."

Shad no sooner finished eating than he heard the

sound of approaching horses. Grabbing his rifle, he stepped to a window.

"McNary's here," he called. "He's brought eight men with him."

Abe joined him at the window. "That ought to be enough to make Hatten sit up and take notice."

They went out to meet the new arrivals. McNary looked tired after having ridden most of the night.

"Are you going to be all right, friend?" Abe asked him.

"Sure," said McNary. "I'm just getting my second wind. Don't worry about me."

Shad went out to the corral and whistled for Squire. The dun trotted over and nuzzled his hand. "I've got some work for you today," he said to the horse. He put the bridle on. Then he threw the saddle over the horse's back and tightened the cinch.

"Ponder," he called to the old man, who was hovering nearby. "I want you to stay here with Kershaw. Keep him out of trouble."

"I'll do 'er," he promised.

It was a lot of responsibility, but Shad couldn't spare anyone else.

"Everyone ready to ride?" he called.

"Ready," said McNary, who should have been the least ready of them all.

Shad and Abe led off. The others fell in behind as they headed north.

The sun was up and shedding its warmth and light over the plains. Under other circumstances, Shad would be enjoying himself, riding across the vast open expanse. But not this morning. Too much was at stake.

It was close to midday when they came up against the first of Hatten's guards. The two rough-looking *hombres* were stationed at the southern edge of the land that Jed Hatten claimed as his own.

"Hold it!" one of them shouted. "Don't come any closer."

"All we want to do is have a little talk with your boss," said Abe, his voice calm and reasonable.

"He don't want to talk to the likes of you. Now turn your horses around and go back where you came from!"

"We've come to get a woman Hatten's been holding at his place against her will. Do you want to be a part of that?"

The guard wasn't moved. "You're crazy! There's no woman being held against her will. Now git!"

"No," said Abe. "We're going on past."

The man wasn't having it. "Oh, no, you ain't!" he yelled, bringing his gun up and pulling the hammer back. Then he noticed that a couple of the M Bar W riders had guns aimed straight at his head.

"Drop your weapons!" Shad ordered Hatten's guards. "Both of you. If you don't, it won't be much trouble to bury you."

Not liking their chances, they did as they were told.

McNary climbed down and gathered their firearms while Shad and Abe bound the two. Then Shad grabbed the reins of their horses.

"You can have 'em back after we leave," he promised. "We'll turn 'em loose."

"You've got a whole lot of nerve going up against Hatten this way," said the one who'd done all the talking. "He'll have all your hides nailed to his barn door—don't think that he won't."

"Your boss took a woman off the stage, and he killed a judge," said Abe. "One of these days he's going to hang. I'm betting that day's not far off."

"Oh, yeah?" said Hatten's man. "We'll see who hangs."

With the guards out of the way, the men rode on to the house. Shad had no way of knowing how many men Hatten would be keeping close by. He might even see some of the Judge's former cowhands. He truly hoped that wouldn't be the case.

Their own number was eleven. Still, they approached Hatten's place with caution. Abe appeared apprehensive. Shad understood. He was worried himself. They were about to meet the woman claiming to be Anne Madison. When they did, they'd know without a doubt that the Judge's daughter, the real one, was either dead or in big trouble.

Chapter Four

Anne had never felt so alone or so frightened in her life as she lay shivering in the darkness. She had no idea where she was being held, but the place smelled musty and unclean. The floor beneath her was nothing but hard-packed dirt, and both her wrists were raw from her struggles with her bindings. Her throbbing head was filled with cobwebs, making it difficult to think. She eased herself back down and willed the cobwebs to clear.

Her troubles had begun when that awful telegram arrived, telling of her father's murder. The shock of it had been too great for tears. Next came the hurried packing for her journey south to Trinidad, a place she knew only from her father's stories. After her trunk was loaded onto the wagon, she'd hugged Aunt Sadie and Uncle Art and climbed up beside Chester, the hired man. He was to drive her to the stage station. But on the way he suddenly turned into an alley between buildings that was barely wide enough to accommodate the team.

"This isn't the way to the station!" she'd cried. "Chester, turn around. You're going to make me late for the stage."

Without a word the hired hand drove into a dark warehouse at the end of the alley.

She remembered jumping off the wagon seat and running for the door, spurred on by fear. But there were others in the warehouse. Before she could make good her escape, they'd grabbed her and pinned her arms to her sides. She was crying out when a rag was held over her face. To her horror it was soaked in chloroform. Then her struggles ceased, and there was nothing but blackness.

Now she was a prisoner. The stage to Trinidad, long gone. *But why? What was this all about? Why had Chester, a trusted hired man, kidnapped her?*

She tried to ignore the throbbing in her head and concentrate. *This has to have something to do with Papa's murder.* According to the telegram from Abe Featherstone, her father had been shot. But the wire didn't name the killer.

She was startled by the sound of small feet scurrying around in the darkness. Another fear presented itself. Rats. She fought back panic and thumped her feet to frighten them away. There was further scurrying, then silence. Anne drew a deep breath of relief.

So many unanswered question whirled around in her

head. But then, she'd suffered unanswered questions for most of her eighteen years. Anger and frustration pushed some of the fear away. Why hadn't her father been open and truthful with her? It simply wasn't fair.

The two of them had enjoyed happy times together. From an early age she was aware that he was a judge. An important man in Colorado. But to her he was simply Father. She'd adored him and looked forward to his visits, which didn't come often enough to suit her. Those had been the sweetest moments of her life. When he left, as he always did, she'd consoled herself with the knowledge that he'd return one day. Then, for another brief time, they could be together again. But a single telegram had put an end to that consolation. Her father was dead. It appeared that whoever killed him intended to get rid of her as well.

She heard the murmur of voices outside her prison. As quietly as possible, she scooted toward the sound and put her ear to a crack in the door to listen.

"Did you go back and tell the Bolins that their niece, or whatever she is, boarded the stage on time?"

"Yeah. It went just like we planned." That was Chester speaking! The first voice was one she didn't recognize.

"Good. Now, the boss wants us to take her down to his place. He figures he might need her for something. Might have to ask her questions, stuff that Gert will have to know."

"Do you think Gert can pass for that skinny, stuck-up girl?" said Chester.

"You saw her. Same hair, blue eyes, and about the same height. Gert's a little older and more filled out, and she's been around the block a few times, but she's a good actress. Besides, none of 'em down at Trinidad has ever laid eyes on the Madison girl. Most they've got is a description."

"Well, I'm pulling up stakes and heading down there with you. I don't want Hatten to forget what he owes me."

"That's fine with me. Just make up some story for the Bolins so they don't get suspicious about your quittin' so sudden-like."

Anne felt a knot of fear in her stomach. They were taking her away from everyone she knew. And when they were done with her, they were going to kill her. These were bad men. The worst. The Judge had told her that many fearsome outlaws respected women and refused to harm them, but these animals had no respect at all.

The door opened then, and she was loaded into the back of a wagon like a bag of grain. The days that followed were each part of a long nightmare. Occasionally the wagon stopped, and she was fed and given water. More than once she was chloroformed. Her captors weren't taking any chances on her escaping.

At last the miserable journey came to an end. When she regained consciousness, she found herself locked in a shed. What followed were hours of worry and boredom. She overheard her captors mention the name

Hatten again. She must be this Hatten's prisoner, somewhere in the vicinity of Trinidad.

Days had passed since she washed or changed her clothes. Because of the chloroform, she wasn't sure how many. She longed for a bath, even a sponge bath, and clean garments from the skin out. But knew she'd be lucky to get decent food and enough water to drink.

It was a sure thing that she couldn't count on any help from Denver. The Bolins believed her to be safe with her guardian, Abe Featherstone. Aunt Sadie and Uncle Art were fine, kind people, and even though her father had paid them well to care for her, she'd come to love them like blood relatives.

She thought of her beautiful, talented mother, Rowena, who'd been an entertainer with a lovely voice. She'd adored her and been devastated by her death. Her father had come from Trinidad toward the end. At the time Anne was a child of eight, and her father's presence had been her only solace.

"Annie, my dear, you look exactly like your mother," Papa had told her. "And you sing like an angel too."

He'd asked her then to sing the haunting tune "Greensleeves," and she saw him wipe his eyes before the song was finished.

"Your mother loved 'Greensleeves,'" he'd said. "But I favor another. You know which one it is."

Of course, she knew. It was the one with her name in it. "Annie Laurie."

The memories of her lost family made her feel even

more alone. If only her father were able to come and take her away from this place. He'd been a strong man who could do anything, and never in her life had she needed him more desperately. Where was Abe Featherstone, the longtime friend her father had trusted more than anyone? And where was that young man he'd taken under his wing? He'd spoken of Shadrach Wakefield often and proudly and regarded him as a son. Could it be that they, too, were part of a conspiracy to rob her? Since she'd never been harmed before, this must be about her inheritance. From what the kidnappers said, she knew that Hatten had hired a woman named Gert to impersonate her. No, she decided, her father's friends would never have taken part in this crime.

When the criminals no longer had use for her, they'd kill her—of that she had no doubt. If only she could find a way to escape.

There was a murmur of voices outside the shed door. With no further warning it swung open, and sunlight pouring in momentarily blinded her. A foul-smelling man entered the shed. He reached down and grabbed her by one arm, dragging her to her feet.

"So this is the high-and-mighty Miss Madison," he taunted.

Her vision adjusted, allowing her to see. The outlaw was mangy-looking, reminding her of a rust-colored feral dog. The smell of him made her queasy. But his eyes were the worst of all. As they stared at her, they betrayed no sign of humanity.

"Good news," he said. "We're going to keep you around for awhile. That is, if you behave yourself."

"You murdered my father," she accused. "I know that you intend to murder me. But you're not going to get away with it."

He shoved her roughly, and she fell to the floor. "Tell me, who's going to stop me?"

Her heart sank, for it was a question she couldn't answer.

"Don't give me any trouble," he warned. "If you try anything, I'll make you wish you hadn't."

Having made the threat, he stalked out and slammed the door behind him. She heard a thud as the bolt fell back into place. In the dim light that filtered through a few cracks in the walls, she searched frantically for something she could use as a weapon. There was nothing. *Someone will come,* she told herself. But it was scant comfort, for she didn't really believe it.

Someone did come later, but it was only to toss in a few blankets. Those and the chamber pail in one corner were the extent of her amenities. Soon after, a man brought food.

After that, food was brought on a regular basis. But, confined in the windowless shed, she felt her sense of time grow foggy.

She believed it was the following morning when she received a visitor. She was alerted by the sound of a woman's strident voice outside the shed.

"I don't care a pile of horse droppings what Jed's orders are," said the unfamiliar voice. "Your Uncle Jed isn't here. I'm here. And I'm going to take a look at the Madison girl. How in blazes am I supposed to do a believable impersonation when I haven't even seen her?"

"Seems to me you did all right yesterday, Gertie."

"Run along, Avery," she said, dismissing him. "Go find somebody else to annoy, and leave me alone."

Avery uttered a string of curses and then said, "When my uncle's not around, I'm the boss. He told me so."

From what Anne could hear, the woman wasn't intimidated.

"Look, you little rodent, you couldn't boss a half-witted mule. Now, open that door, and get out of here."

"Tuck, stand guard," Avery ordered. "Don't let her do anything my uncle wouldn't approve of."

Anne heard the sound of the bolt being removed. She got to her feet, for it appeared that she was about to meet her impersonator face-to-face.

The woman who entered the shed could pass for Anne's older sister. Her hair was almost the same color, her eyes were blue, and she was the same height. But there was a hardness to her expression. The beginnings of lines at the mouth and eyes. A look of discontent. Anne was being appraised as well.

"You don't appear to be so classy after all," said the woman called Gertie. "But then, you haven't been pampered in awhile."

If Gertie harbored any kindness or compassion, she kept it hidden.

"How much are they paying you to steal my identity and my inheritance?" Anne asked.

A flash of anger crossed the older woman's face. "None of your business," she said. "And you might ought to watch your mouth."

Anne seized the chance to plant a seed of doubt. "We both know that your friend Hatten is a murderer. Do you ever wonder how he plans to pay you off after you've done your job and he doesn't need you anymore?"

In the dim light of the shed she could see Gertie scowl.

"Look, I'm not some kind of hired hand," Gert said. "Jed's going to marry me as soon as I inherit that ranch he wants. I'll clean him up a little, teach him some manners, and we'll soon be one of the most respected families in the area, not to mention the richest."

"Has it occurred to you that Hatten needn't be married long in order to become a rich widower?" Anne asked.

By Gertie's expression, Anne could tell that she'd hit a nerve.

"Jed would never do anything to hurt me," she protested. "He loves me. Now, shut up before I order Tuck to give you another whiff of that chloroform. Or even better, a clout on the head."

The harshness of her response made Anne suspect that Gert already had doubts about Hatten's intentions. Doubts she didn't want to admit.

"Turn around," Gertie ordered.

Anne did so, not knowing what to expect. She felt the woman scrutinizing her.

"You're on the skinny side, but the match is close enough."

"How did you come to learn about me?" Anne inquired. "My existence was a well-guarded secret."

Gertie laughed. "That fool Bolin likes to run off at the mouth at the local saloons when he's in his cups. You've not been a secret since he started drinking Saturday nights at the Golden Horseshoe."

So, Uncle Art had caused all this. Still, he'd not betrayed her on purpose. That, at least, was a comfort.

"Jed and Avery were up in Denver having some fun," said the woman. "Avery happened to overhear Bolin talking about the Judge and his daughter. For once, he had sense enough to do the smart thing. He passed the word along to Jed. It's about the first and last smart thing he's ever done."

"So after learning who my father was, Hatten came up with the plan to kill him and hire you as my replacement."

"Beautiful, no? Not only that, he figured out a way to put the blame on some ne'er-do-well saloon swamper who'd threatened Madison's life in front of witnesses. It would have worked, too, if the stupid man had done what he was supposed to and died. But he got himself taken alive, and he talked. At least he talked to Featherstone and Wakefield. Jed's plan still has a good chance to work, though. He's got half the county thinking that them two went and hired Barney Kershaw to kill Madison for his land and money."

Anne was sickened by the evil of Hatten's scheme. The man was a true scoundrel. But the local people surely knew something of her father's friends. How could any of them believe those awful lies? Still, she was aware that lies could be spoken and spread with great effectiveness.

Gertie checked her watch brooch. "I've got to get out of here before Jed gets back. Enjoy yourself while you can, Miss Madison. Your understudy won't need you much longer."

It was a clear warning to Anne that she was marked for death.

Gert knocked on the door for Tuck to let her out. Then, in a swish of skirts, she was gone, leaving behind the faint scent of perfume.

Anne sank to the floor in despair. There was simply no way to escape the confines of the shed.

If only she had the power to turn back the clock to the day before that hateful telegram arrived. She'd find a way to warn her father and give him the chance to be armed and ready. Had he been prepared, he would have survived, and she would be safe and happy with him now. Hatten would be the one who was dead.

She acknowledged that the predicament she found herself in was partly her own fault. She had trusted Chester too readily. She should have paid closer attention to his odd behavior. He'd always had sneaky mannerisms, like pulling his hat low over his face whenever he accompanied her to town. No doubt there was a WANTED dodger with his likeness on it. When he'd turned down that alley, she should have jumped out of the wagon immediately. Started screaming, even. Instead, she'd gone with him quietly, like a lamb to the slaughter. But she had no power to change the past, and now she was going to die for her mistakes.

The next time the guard brought her a plate of food, she had no appetite.

"Better eat," he urged. "You'll need your strength."

She looked up at the scruffy, hard-bitten man and saw pity in his eyes. Of course, he would know what her fate was to be.

"Would you want to be guilty of killing a woman, Tuck?" she asked.

"No, ma'am, I surely wouldn't. There's more'n one of us wouldn't."

"That's what your boss is going to do. You know that, don't you?"

He shifted his weight from one foot to the other and looked uncomfortable. "I'm sorry, ma'am, I truly am, but I ain't got no say in what he does. He pays me and gives me orders. I follow 'em."

"Then you can't help me?"

"Afraid not. But I'm sorry as I can be."

She nodded in acknowledgment of his apology. Tuck would be of no help. Maybe he wouldn't fire the bullet that killed her, but he was willing to stand by and let someone else do it.

"Go ahead," Tuck urged. "Try to eat, ma'am."

He left her then and closed the door behind him. She took the fork and picked at the tasteless food. Tuck was right: she did need her strength. The daughter of Harley Madison was going down fighting to her very last breath.

It was the next day that Anne heard the riders. She rushed to the small crack in the boards that she used for a peephole. Part of her view was blocked, but she could see an older man out in front of the others. Her heart started pounding. Maybe they'd come to rescue her. She had to let them know that she was here.

Suddenly the door flew open. Before she could scream, the guard had a hand over her mouth and was pinning her arms to her sides. She kicked his legs and struggled to get free, but his grip was like iron, and he held her fast. She couldn't even witness what was going on between the riders and her captors. The guard who'd replaced Tuck looked out through her peephole. All Anne could do was listen.

Chapter Five

When Hatten's place came into view, it was nothing more than a run-down shack thrown together with weathered boards. It reminded Shad of a dirty gray fungus sprouting from the earth. Absent was the craftsmanship that had gone into the building of the Judge's house, as well as his own. As they approached, he could smell the stench from a refuse pile beside the sagging porch. He wondered what the woman, whoever she was, thought of her new living quarters.

Since the boundary guards had been trusted to stop intruders, Shad and his men were able to get close before the alarm went up. Then came a shout, and Hatten's men appeared from different places, ready to defend their boss. The glint of sunlight on a rifle barrel alerted Shad to the man positioned in the loft of the unfinished barn. Eight men in all, he counted. No doubt

Hatten was inside the shack with the woman and the Ute cook. Probably the nephew, Avery, was in there as well.

"There's one in the loft," he said softly to Abe. "Take care."

"I see him," came the reply.

Slowly and deliberately they rode in. Shad's nerves were taut, and he was prepared for action.

"Hold it right there!" yelled a voice from inside the house. A rifle barrel poked through an open window. "You're trespassing on my land. I want every last one of you to turn around and get out of here! Right now!"

Shad glimpsed the speaker at the window—rusty beard, bulbous nose—enough to know it was Hatten himself who was doing the shouting. The man looked nothing like his comely nephew. *Ordinary* was how Kershaw had described him.

Shad's men held their ground. Abe stepped his mount to a forward position.

"Now, look here, Hatten," he said, "I've come to fetch home my ward, Miss Anne Madison. It ain't proper for her to be up here, and you know it. I'm surprised at your behavior."

There was a long pause. It was plain to everyone that the numbers on both sides were about equal. If anyone opened fire, there was sure to be a lot of bloodshed. Out of the corner of his eye Shad watched the man in the barn loft.

"Anne's staying right where she is, Featherstone. She ain't about to go off with a couple of killers like you and Wakefield!"

Abe winced as if he'd been struck a blow. "Then she sure as sin doesn't want to stay here," he said. "We know it was you who murdered the Judge."

"Liar!" came the voice of a woman from inside.

While they watched, she flounced onto the porch. Her hair was the color of honey, and her stylish green dress hugged her curvaceous figure. But her appearance was marred by her expression. In addition to the anger that distorted her features, there was a hardness around her mouth and eyes. She also looked to be a lot older than Anne Madison's eighteen years. The words *worldly* and *jaded* came to Shad's mind.

"Say what you will," she said, glaring at Abe, "but you're no guardian of mine. You and Wakefield went out and hired that killer, Kershaw, to shoot my father. I'm not going to rest until I see all three of you hang."

She's rehearsed that little speech well, thought Shad.

"Anne, that's just not true," said Abe, as if he believed the woman to be the real thing. "We were loyal friends to Judge Madison. His real killer is right there on that porch, hiding behind your skirts."

Hatten had stepped out behind her, gun drawn. Now he put his left hand on her waist in a proprietorial way.

"Get out!" she yelled. "All of you! Right now!"

"You heard my bride-to-be," said the outlaw. "Get out of here while you're still able to ride."

Hatten knew he was safe enough, Shad mused. His men wouldn't fire on Jed and risk hitting a woman, no matter how obnoxious she was. Her pretended naïvété disgusted Shad. The woman on the porch was no more related to Harley Madison than to Queen Victoria.

Abe tried again. "Anne, I don't know what's come over you. You can't be serious about hitching up with that skunk."

She put her hands over her ears. "Go away, you awful man," she said. "I refuse to listen to any more of your vicious lies."

Shad saw the smirk on Hatten's face. He looked as if he'd just dragged in the biggest pot in the poker game.

"The lady has spoke her piece," he said. "Now, I won't say it again. All of you, get off my land!"

"Come on," urged McNary. "There's nothing more we can do here. The lady, whoever she is, has been warned."

"Then let's leave careful-like," said Abe.

They backed their horses away, all the while keeping watch on the armed outlaws. Shad was especially wary of the one hidden in the loft. When they'd reached a safe distance, they wheeled and rode off.

When they were well away from Hatten's spread, Abe voiced his opinion. "If I ever had doubts, I sure don't have any now. That woman back there wasn't Anne Madison. I didn't even need to use my test. Not only is she a lot older, but I could tell by the way she looked and acted that Harley Madison had nothing at all to do with her upbringing."

"The question is," said McNary, "what happened to the real one?"

"I don't want to think about it," said Abe. "Not right now, anyway."

Shad knew that his friend feared the worst had happened to the girl. On the way back to the Lazy M he tried to think of reasons Hatten might keep Anne Madison alive. The only one he could come up with was the imposter's need for a coach. Questions might be asked that only the real Anne could answer. But once the older woman had been accepted by the community, Anne would then be dispensable.

"You've got to admit that it's a smart move," said McNary, "Hatten marrying the heir to the Judge's fortune. Everything will be his if he can pass her off as the real thing."

In Shad's opinion, the outlaw could have found a closer match. But maybe others around Trinidad wouldn't look on the imposter with such a critical eye.

"The sheriff ought to be told about this," said Abe. "When we get back to the ranch, I'm going to ride into town and have a talk with Baca. I don't care who Hatten's got out there to keep us away."

"I'll go with you," said Shad. "But if Toby got through with my note, Baca already has an idea about what's going on."

"Just the same, I'd rather tell it all face-to-face. See if I can get him to help us find Anne. The real one."

It wasn't until Anne heard the horses ride away that the guard released her, shoving her roughly to the floor. Without a word he left and bolted the door behind him.

Anne sat there in stunned silence. Rescue had been so close and yet so impossible. If she was going to survive, she would have to do it on her own.

It was late by the time Shad and the others got back to the Lazy M. They could tell that Toby had returned from his mission in Trinidad, for Banjo was in the corral. They found Toby himself inside with Ponder. The nervous Kershaw was with them. He'd stayed put in their absence.

"Lark managed to get your message to Sheriff Baca right away," said Toby. "He sent one back." The kid pulled a scrap of paper from his hatband and handed it over for Shad to read.

"What's it say?" asked Abe.

"Bad news, I'm afraid. We're on our own. The sheriff says there's nothing he can do without evidence. Besides, Hatten's statement has gotten around, and public opinion is turning against us."

Abe grimaced. "Should have known. That's about what I figured on."

"Oh, there's something I forgot to tell you," said Toby.

"Well, spit it out, boy."

"This wasn't in the note. But Baca's wired some different places with Hatten's description, asking for information. He said not to count on anything, but you never know. He told Lark that it's not going to get out that he done this, either, 'cause he threatened Hernandez at the telegraph office with a life of misery if it does. If anything comes of it, he'll send word."

This boosted Shad's respect for the elected official. It appeared he actually was trying to do his job.

"Should I keep some of the men here in case we need them?" said McNary. "Or should I send them all back to the M Bar W?"

Shad considered their situation. The Judge had at least a few hundred head of cattle out on the range. Hatten might be using this opportunity to add some of them to his own herd. They ought to be checked. Then there were the usual chores to do. Ponder was still recovering from the blow he'd received, and with an enemy to the north, they might need men on short notice. As it stood, he had only Abe, McNary, and Toby to rely on. He didn't even bother to count Kershaw.

"Have Dobbs and Montoya stay," he said. "Rutledge and Lemke too. Send the others back to the ranch. They'll be needed there. Then get yourself some sleep. You look like you could use it."

McNary hurried off to relay the order while Ponder stirred up a meal.

Toby took over the Judge's chair and propped his heels on the overstuffed footstool. Abe and Shad sprawled on the floor in front of the fireplace.

"I guess you couldn't get that girl to leave Hatten," said Toby.

"Nope," said Abe. "I don't know who she is, but she's in cahoots with 'im. Intends to inherit the ranch and turn it over to Hatten when he marries her."

"Do tell. What about the real daughter?"

The question brought a stricken look to Abe's face.

"We don't know where she is," said Shad. "I don't think she's dead. They still need her to coach the imposter."

"What if she was out there all that time?" said Abe.

That had crossed Shad's mind as well. "Look, if we'd made a move, they'd probably have killed her," he said. "Don't torture yourself with how things might be and what we might've done."

"Yeah, you need to be worrying about your own selves," said Toby. "I overheard some talk when I was in Trinidad. Not everyone's against you, but there's some loudmouths who want to string you up, and they're trying to poison people's minds about you."

Shad felt sick at heart. He'd known many of those people ever since he could remember. His father had been murdered while serving as their sheriff, and it was hurtful to learn that a lie started by Hatten and the imposter could turn even a few against him.

"What I want to know is," Toby continued, "how come the Judge kept his daughter a secret?"

Abe's expression softened as his thoughts went back in time. "Well, son, I first learned about her when the Judge made me her guardian—'just in case anything should happen,' he said. That must have been ten or eleven years back. It was right after her mother's death. The poor woman came down with an illness that took her quick. I recall that a friend in Denver sent word for Harley to come, said that a 'valued friend' was real bad sick. He dropped everything and hurried to her side. A couple named Bolin took care of the little girl until he could get there. He liked the way they'd done, so he asked them to keep her and raise her for him. They agreed to do it. I know that he sent them money on a regular basis. He even paid for a year of Anne's schooling at one of them fancy female academies in the East."

"Why didn't he bring the girl's mother down here to Trinidad?" Shad inquired.

Abe sighed. "That might seem sensible to you or to me, but not to the Judge. You see, Rowena was an entertainer. She was singing in a Denver saloon when they met. Mind you, she wasn't one of them 'soiled doves.' However, I'm told that she wore mighty colorful outfits that were a little skimpy at the top. She also used a bit of rouge. All in all, the so-called respectable ladies would have shunned her. Rowena was real pretty, from what I've heard. Lots of menfolk came to hear her sing. The Judge was one of 'em. They got to seeing each other every chance they could, and eventually they got married in secret. Trouble was, Rowena was fairly well known, and she wasn't engaged in a profession that was suitable for a politician's wife. Especially one with high-flung ambitions like Harley."

"If this Rowena was so unsuitable, then he shouldn't have married her," said Toby.

Abe sighed. "A man does strange things for love, my boy," he said. "He wanted her for himself even if he had to live two lives in order to keep her. Things didn't change when his daughter was born."

"Seems he'd have wanted Anne to know him," said Shad. "To have some kind of family feeling."

"Oh, he visited his little girl as often as he could get away. You may recall all those trips he made to Denver on one pretext or another."

Shad did remember. The Judge would pack his bags and go off for a visit to old friends, or to see a play, or to have some suits tailored.

"Rowena understood and accepted their arrangement," said Abe. "But I wonder if the child ever did."

It struck Shad as ironic that Anne's father had to die before she was summoned home. As things stood, she might not ever make it.

"I don't intend to hole up out here like a prairie dog while Hatten plays his game," Shad said, getting to his feet. "I'm going to ride into town first thing tomorrow and talk to Baca in person. Let him know that a young woman is in trouble. If the townspeople have anything to say, let them say it to my face."

"I'm going to be right beside you," said Abe. "I want to see my wife. I don't like it that she's alone in town with bad feelings running like they are. Besides, Baca might have gotten some answers to his wires."

"It might be a good idea for you to bring Lark back to the ranch," said Shad. "Out here we can do a better job of protecting her."

"I'll do it. No sense in taking any chances."

After they'd eaten and seen to the stock, they came in and bedded down near the fireplace. McNary and the rest of the M Bar W hands were out at the bunkhouse. Shad noticed that Kershaw wasn't acting quite so hopeless as before. It appeared he was taking heart from the fact that they knew who the Judge's real killer was. He was lucky that they hadn't shot him. Real lucky. And, doubtless, no one was more aware of this than Kershaw.

Lemke and Ponder had been assigned the first watch. Shad wasn't taking any chances on a surprise attack. Tomorrow he would try to make it past the outlaws who were charged with stopping him. Then he'd light a fire under Sheriff Baca.

Chapter Six

When they started for Trinidad, it was a little past dawn. Shad rode the *grullo,* giving Squire a needed rest. Abe was astride the blood bay. They were ready for trouble.

"I'm betting that Hatten's still got someone watching for us," said Abe. "That coyote won't want us telling folks what really happened. A lot of 'em would be mighty interested in what we have to say."

"No doubt you're right," he agreed.

The sun rose higher and warmed the land as they covered the distance toward town. Shad shrugged out of his coat and paused long enough to fasten it behind the cantle.

"You know, Abe, I've been thinking about Hatten's past. A man like that has got to have left a trail. I suspect Baca is going to get some interesting answers to his wires."

"That's likely so," Abe agreed. "And, unless I miss my guess, that woman up there with him has left some tracks too. The way she looks and acts, she's got to have been around some."

From what McNary had told him, and from what he'd seen and heard with his own eyes and ears, he was betting Abe was right.

"It might be a good idea to have Baca send out some inquiries on her as well."

He had to admit that the imposter would make a pretty fair actress. *What if she'd had a lot of practice already? What if she was skilled at various confidence games?*

"The way I figure it," said Abe, "Hatten and his nephew hatched themselves a scheme that almost worked. If we hadn't been able to take Kershaw alive in that canyon so he could tell his story, and if their impersonator had been a little younger and a lot more of a lady, they'd have pulled it off."

Shad inwardly shuddered to think how things might have been if they'd gone the way Hatten had intended. He recalled something the Judge had once told him about criminal schemes. "The best of them often go off course, Shadrach, because there's simply too many unforseen things that can happen." This scheme was ill-conceived to begin with. It had included murder.

Shad stayed alert as they drew nearer to town.

"Well, I don't see anybody yet," said Abe, looking

over the landscape. "But that doesn't mean they're not out there. A sniper could be lying belly-down in the grass, and he'd be hard to see."

It wasn't until the land sloped upward, creating a small rise, that they spotted a lone man on horseback. He appeared to be waiting.

"Uh-oh," said Abe. "I reckon this is it."

"At least there's only one."

They rode straight ahead, never lessening their pace. To Shad's left Fisher's Peak rose like a sentinel from the valley of the Purgatoire. Far to the west lay the fabled Spanish Peaks.

Hatten's man held his ground. He appeared to be young, younger than Shad. A pistol was stuck in his belt, and a rifle rode in his saddle scabbard.

"Hold up there," he ordered. "Both of you turn around and go on back where you came from."

About thirty yards separated them now.

"Seems to me it's a free country, son," said Abe, his tone amiable. "My friend and I have a notion to go into town. My wife lives there, and she's waiting for me. I don't want to worry her none."

His mild response caused the outlaw to hesitate. "Look, I've got my orders. I know you're from the M Bar W, and I'm not supposed to let you pass."

"Who gave those orders, son?"

"My boss, Jed Hatten."

"Well, I can understand that. Your boss don't want us telling it around Trinidad about how he murdered Judge Madison, or how he framed an innocent man for that murder and set him up to get killed. If we go in there telling what really happened, your boss is apt to be stretching hemp."

The young outlaw looked miserable. Saddle leather creaked as he shifted his weight. But would he yield? The .44 felt heavy on Shad's hip.

"Like I said, I can't let you pass. I've got my orders."

"Well, the man who gave 'em to you is a murderer," said Abe. "Do you really want to be a part of what he's doing?"

While his partner tried to talk their way out of the predicament, Shad was mentally preparing for a showdown. In their favor, Hatten's man was looking east, into the sun. Not only that, he was alone against the two of them. The young outlaw had to be considering his disadvantages.

Shad waited, his hand inches away from his pistol.

Their opponent struggled to reach a decision. "Oh, go on into town if you've a mind to," he said at last. "I don't care. Hatten's not paying me enough to die for him."

"A wise decision," said Abe. "It means you'll live another day."

"Suppose you ride along with us," said Shad. "I wouldn't like to tempt you into shooting us in the back."

The outlaw's face flushed red. "I'm not that kind," he said. "There's a limit to what I'll do. But, sure, I'll ride along with you."

While he had the chance, Shad questioned him about the Judge's murder.

"Look, I don't know anything about it," he said. "They don't tell me nothin', and I don't stick my neck out and ask questions. It's not healthy. All I know is, the boss described both of you and ordered me to stop you from going into town. I was told to do whatever it took, even shoot you if necessary. Trouble is, I'm no killer, and I sure don't want to die."

The big rawboned kid was clearly new to Hatten's way of doing things. He had no stomach for killing and actually seemed basically decent. Maybe his only mistake was signing on with the wrong outfit.

"Look," said Abe, "if you're as smart as I think you are, you won't stick around. Hatten's killed a man, and too many people know it. We suspect he may have killed a woman too. Sooner or later he's going to hang. If I were you, I wouldn't want to be standing too close to him. In your place, I'd head out for New Mexico."

The kid thought it over, then nodded. "I expect you're right. I'm mostly a cowhand, not an outlaw. Fact is, that's what Hatten hired me for. To punch cows. Instead, I end up doing his dirty work. He owes me back wages, but I guess he can keep 'em."

"If you're short," said Abe, "I've got a few dollars you can have. I hate to see a man cheated out of what he's earned."

The kid's face brightened. "I'll take 'em and be obliged. Maybe someday I can pay it back."

Shad didn't think that was too likely, but it sounded polite.

"I've got one question first," said Abe as he pulled some bills from his vest pocket. "Have you seen the Madison girl Hatten's been keeping out at his place?"

He scowled. "Everybody around there has. More'n that, we've heard her. That woman is squawking about something all the time. She can't mind her own business for shucks. Truth to tell, I was glad to get away from there."

"What does Hatten do about her?"

"Mostly he ignores her."

"She doesn't sound like the kind of girl who'd be related to the Judge," said Shad.

"If you're saying she's no lady, then you're right. She uses language that would make a man blush."

Abe looked grim.

"By any chance, did you happen to see another girl out there?" said Shad.

"Nope. But that's not saying there ain't one."

Shad sensed the man knew something he was holding back. "What do you mean?" he said.

"Well, I heard a couple of the hands talking in the bunkhouse. They claimed they saw the boss and his nephew bringing somebody in late one night. Whoever it was, they had 'em covered up pretty good. They put 'em in the shed that's farthest from the house and bolted the door. Posted a guard too. Shed was still being guarded when I rode out. Nobody gets close to that place without the boss's say-so."

Shad glanced at his partner. Abe had an angry look on his face. At the same time, it must have given him hope that his ward was still alive.

"Have you got a name, son?" Abe inquired.

"Hobart. Tom Hobart. I don't know how I let myself get mixed up with that bunch in the first place. So far I've got no trouble with the law, but you're right. If I stick around Hatten much longer, that'll change."

"Then I guess you know what you need to do."

"Yeah, I know. I'm going to stop in town long enough to pick up some grub. Then I'll ride south. If you run into Hatten or any of his outfit, I'd take it kindly if you didn't mention my name."

"You can count on that," said Abe. "Good luck to you."

They parted company with Hobart before entering town and let him go ahead. It wouldn't do for him to be seen with them. After waiting a spell, they followed. It didn't take long for them to notice a change in Trinidad. They garnered several hostile looks as they rode down the main street. A woman Shad recognized as the blacksmith's wife put her hands on her hips and glared at them as they passed by. Obviously Hatten's story had taken root in at least some minds, allowing people to believe that greed had overcome friendship, and the scheme to get rid of the Judge and put the blame on Kershaw was Shad and Abe's own. He recalled with shame his own readiness to accept Kershaw's guilt and to hunt him down in anger. He'd even considered Abe's skepticism foolish.

"Nice friendly place, ain't it?" Abe commented, his voice heavy with sarcasm.

"It's been friendlier."

They hitched their horses in front of the jail and went inside. Sheriff Baca's head was bowed over some papers he was signing. When he heard them enter, he looked up.

Seeing who it was, he frowned. "I didn't expect you *hombres* would be coming into town anytime soon. Señora Featherstone delivered your note."

"We wouldn't be here," said Abe, "if Hatten had had his way about it. We ran into a man he had posted to stop us. He was ordered to kill us if we didn't turn back."

Baca's eyebrows went up a fraction. "I had no idea," he said. "Since you're here, did you have to shoot him?"

"Nope. The young fellow we ran into decided there was a better way to make a living. He's had his fill of Hatten's orders, and he took off for New Mexico."

"I must say I'm glad to hear that. It means one less problem for Colorado."

Shad figured Baca had his troubles.

"Have a chair," the sheriff invited, indicating the two across from his desk. Abe took the one that was closest. Shad pulled up the other.

"Cigar?" asked Baca, offering them an open box. They both declined.

The sheriff eased back in his chair, clipped the end of one for himself, and lit it. With his first puff, smoke crossed the space that separated them. The tobacco scent brought back a nostalgic memory of the Judge, who'd enjoyed a good cigar from time to time.

"I guess you've heard that the story is spreading that you two hired Kershaw to kill Judge Madison," said Baca. "Hatten swears he overhead you hiring that saloon swamper to do it. He made it sound so convincing that more than a few are starting to believe it. They figure that either you didn't know about the daughter or that you planned to do away with her before she could claim her inheritance. I've been bombarded with complaints. Folks want me to arrest you."

Abe muttered a curse under his breath.

"You get any replies to your telegrams?" asked Shad.

"As a matter of fact," said Baca, "I've received a couple of interesting ones. It seems that Jed Hatten was arrested for stealing stock back in Independence, Missouri. Unfortunately, he disappeared before his trial, along with two of the mayor's finest horses.

"Later he was involved in an altercation in Denver, where he shot a man. Witnesses said Hatten provoked the incident, but the man was wearing a sidearm, so the law didn't make much fuss about it. My friend in Denver told me something interesting, though. He said that Hatten had a pretty blond woman with him at the time. She fits the description of the woman who got off the stage."

"She's got to be the one he's passing off as Anne," said Abe. "No doubt they've been in cahoots for a long time."

"When did this shooting incident happen?" asked Shad.

"According to my friend, a little over a year ago."

"Maybe that's when they discovered the Judge had a daughter," he said. "It was a big secret around here, but it might not have been so well kept up there in Denver, where his wife had lots of friends and admirers."

Baca nodded. "Likely so."

"Sheriff, I've been meaning to ask," said Abe, "did you get a good look at that woman when she got off the stage?"

"Yes. I made it a point to do so. I like to get a look at all the strangers who come to town. She was nicely dressed, and I guess you'd say she was pretty in a way. But she seemed very worldly to me. Not at all what I'd have expected."

"That was my impression too," said Abe. "We took some of the boys and rode up to Hatten's place to bring her home. But she wouldn't have it. Told us off."

"I had occasion to go to Hatten's place once," said Baca. "That shack he lives in looks like a trash heap. Hard to imagine a woman choosing that place over the Judge's ranch."

Shad had thought the exact same thing.

"Hatten made an announcement while we were there," said Abe. "He said that him and this woman he's passing off as Anne Madison were going to get married. She didn't deny it."

Baca blew out a puff of smoke. "The plot becomes ever clearer. Marry the woman and inherit her inheritance."

The sheriff had it figured out. Maybe the town folk Hatten had hoodwinked would get the message too, Shad mused.

"There's more," said Shad. "The fellow who quit Hatten's outfit told us his boss spirited a prisoner to the ranch one night. I think it might be the real Anne Madison. He said that whoever it was is locked in a shed that's guarded all the time."

Baca frowned. This was something he obviously didn't want to hear.

"We're going back up there to get her out."

The sheriff leaned forward. "I understand your concern," he said, "but you're asking for trouble, and I can't help you. Not without proof of a crime. I'm way shorthanded, and there's some powerful citizens against you. Hatten even sent one of his men to complain about your outfit harassing his fiancée. Now, I'm not going to do anything about that, but I expect Hatten will if he gets the chance. I warn you, if you go back to his place, his men will be laying for you."

"Exactly when did that man who complained arrive?" asked Shad.

"Yesterday. Right around noon."

"That was about the time we got to Hatten's place. Before that we'd never laid eyes on the woman. The man's a liar."

"I wouldn't doubt it," said Baca. "But Hatten's pressing his advantage."

Shad was concerned about the real Anne Madison

and how long Hatten would allow her to live. If the substitute passed muster, Anne's death warrant was as good as signed.

"I know that the Judge left a will," said Abe. "Martin Brent was the attorney who took care of it. Reckon it's been read yet?"

"Not to my knowledge. Maybe because you were both away and Brent felt you should be present. Do you know, for sure, who will inherit the Judge's property?"

"I'm guessing that his daughter gets everything, which I wouldn't mind at all under other circumstances. But I sure hate to think all he worked for will end up in Hatten's hands. If it does, the Judge will be turning over in his grave."

"No doubt," said Baca. "He was a strong-willed man with a finely honed sense of justice. Hatten, on the other hand, is scum."

"I wonder whose side Brent is taking in this matter," said Shad. "Do you suppose he thinks we're killers too?"

"I can't say for sure," said Baca. "But he strikes me as a sensible man, and he knows you fairly well. Perhaps you should have a private word with him."

"Good idea," Abe approved. "While Shad does that, I'm going to send a wire to those folks Anne lived with up in Denver. Maybe they can tell us something."

"I wish I could be of more help," said the sheriff. "But my hands are tied. Only a few people in this town have turned against you, but they have considerable influence, including my political opponent. If I were to take my deputies up to Hatten's, they'd say I was derelict in my duty to the people here in town, that I was aiding killers, and that'd sure defeat me in the coming election."

"That's about what I expected," said Abe. "I'm glad that at least you never had any doubts about us."

Baca pulled a saucer toward him and dropped an ash into it. "I had questions from the beginning, not doubts," he said. "For instance, why would an *hombre* like Kershaw murder the one person in this town who'd helped him? Why would a foster son betray his guardian, and why would a man whose loyalty has been proven again and again turn on his friend and destroy him? There was only one answer. They didn't. Add to that the fact that I've never liked Hatten's arrogant, disrespectful manner."

Abe got up and shook the sheriff's hand. "You're a wise man, Baca, and a good one. I think I'll go over to the telegraph office now and have Hernandez send that wire to the Bolins."

"Good idea," said the sheriff. "I, too, have more wires to send. I'm curious about the blond woman. I agree with you that she likely has a past."

"We'd appreciate it if you'd let us know what you find out about her," said Abe.

"I'll do that as soon as I hear. Now you'd best pay a visit to Señora Featherstone as well. She's mighty concerned about your welfare."

"I plan to do that as soon as I finish my business with Hernandez."

After leaving the jail, they went straight to the tele-graph office. From there they went to Abe's place.

Lark heard them ride up, and she ran to meet them, her calico apron flapping in the wind. "I've been so worried," she said as she enfolded Abe in her arms. "There's been some ugly talk."

"I'm sorry you're being put through this," said Abe. "Not everyone has turned against us by a long shot, and I expect the ones who have are going to feel like fools when the truth comes out. It's the Judge's girl I'm wor-ried about."

"Me too," she said. Then she turned to Shad. "It's good to see you, especially the way things are going. I'm glad Abe has you with him."

"Has anybody been treating you wrong?" he asked.

"Nothing more than a glare or a cold shoulder—so far. I heard how Jed Hatten took Anne Madison right off the stage as soon as it arrived. She announced to everyone within hearing who she was, which shocked a lot of folks. That awful man told her how he'd heard you and Abe hiring Kershaw to kill the Judge. Then, after she'd made some nasty comments and demanded your arrest, she went off with him and his men to his ranch."

Shad's jaw clenched as he heard the story again. He wanted to see Hatten hang.

"That woman wasn't the real Anne Madison," he said. "Before one of Hatten's men left his service and took off for New Mexico, he told us that his boss has a prisoner out at his place. Abe and I suspect that prisoner is the Judge's daughter."

A look of horror spread across Lark's face.

"Before we knew anything about a prisoner, we took some of the men and rode up there," said Abe. "The woman he paraded on the porch couldn't possibly be any kin to Harley Madison.

"Can't you get the sheriff to help you free that poor girl?" she asked.

Abe shook his head. "Not without more to go on. Baca has enemies, and he's getting a lot of criticism because he doesn't have us locked up in his jail right now."

She failed to hide her disgust. "They elect a sheriff, they should let him do his job."

"True enough," said Abe, "but right now you have a couple of hungry men to feed."

"What am I thinking?" she said. "Here I am talking, and you must be starved. Come on inside."

Shad had always liked visiting the little adobe house. It had a feeling of snugness and comfort. Abe had kept it clean and neat during his bachelor years, but Lark had added feminine touches, like gingham curtains and a framed sketch of the mountains.

She got busy with the frying pan. Soon there was a platter of bacon and eggs on the table, accompanied by thick slabs of bread. Both of them ate like hungry wolves. When they were finished, Lark sat down and told them what was on her mind.

"I think it would be wise for me to go back to the ranch with you. There are a few hotheads around here stirring up trouble. They might use me to get to you."

"I've been thinking along the same line," said Abe. "Why don't you hurry and get packed. I'll get the buggy ready."

"While you're doing that," said Shad, "I'm going to go have a talk with Martin Brent. I want to hear what he has to say about all this."

What his reception would be, he didn't know. He went out and mounted the *grullo*. Taking a back way, he rode to the lawyer's office, which faced the main street. He tied the horse in the alley and entered through the rear door.

Brent's skinny, bespectacled assistant looked up, startled by his sudden appearance. "What are you doing in here?" he demanded to know.

"I simply want to speak with your boss for a few minutes."

Upon hearing Shad's voice, Martin Brent stepped out of his office. He was a distinguished-looking man in his mid-thirties. There was still no sign of gray in his hair, nor did he have an expanding waistline. He was a widower whose two young children were being reared by his unmarried sister.

"Somehow I figured you'd be dropping by, Wakefield," he said. "Step into my office. We need to have a talk."

He held the door open for Shad to enter and closed it behind him. The room was elegantly furnished, with a large mahogany desk as the centerpiece. There were four leather-covered chairs, counting the one behind the desk. The walls were lined with bookshelves that were filled with law books. Shad noticed the pleasant mingled smells of leather and beeswax polish. Had he chosen to practice law, as he'd been trained to do, he would now have an office much like this one.

"Have a seat," the lawyer invited.

"First off," said Shad, easing himself into the nearest chair, "the rumors about Featherstone and I hiring a killer to shoot the Judge are barefaced lies."

Brent fixed him with a look. "Of course they are. I've known you and Abe far too long to believe otherwise. I don't think for a minute that Kershaw shot him either. Harley became a good and generous friend to him, and only a fool destroys a friend."

Shad relaxed a bit. He was in the presence of an ally. "We know that Jed Hatten killed the Judge," he said.

The lawyer didn't look surprised. "Of course. It had to be. There was no other reason for Hatten to lie. I'm also aware that he was harassing Harley to sell his land."

"For a pitiful price, from what I heard," said Shad. "It got the Judge all riled up. He ran him off."

"I can just see that," said Brent. "No one liked to incur the Judge's wrath. When he was mad, he could beat you to death with his tongue."

Shad smiled, for he'd seen Judge Madison let loose from time to time. They all had.

"I don't think that woman he paraded around is the

Judge's daughter either," said Brent. "Hatten picked the wrong actress. She'd be better cast as a barmaid."

"Maybe she was all he could get," said Shad. "Baca found out they were together up in Denver about a year ago when Hatten shot a man."

"I see. Is Hatten wanted?"

"Not for the shooting. He provoked it, no doubt, but the victim was found to have a sidearm, so nothing was done."

"Self-defense," said Brent, nodding. "Thinly disguised murder, in other words."

"So it would seem. He did steal some horses back in Missouri. I don't know if the warrant is still out or not."

"And the woman?"

"Baca is checking. He thinks she might be wanted. Most likely for confidence schemes."

"Well, don't get discouraged," said Brent. "You have more loyal friends around here than you realize. The others are apt to change their tune when Hatten's past comes out, and that of the woman."

"Good to hear," he said. "We have reason to believe that the real Anne Madison is being held prisoner out at Hatten's place. I'm afraid that the minute you and the others accept the imposter, Anne will be killed."

"Don't worry, I'm not about to accept her. I intend to ask all kinds of questions. I might even send for the people she stayed with in Denver. At least that's a threat I can hold over her."

Brent was smart.

"Good. I wouldn't want to end up partners in the M Bar W with the likes of her and that killer."

Brent leaned back in his chair and steepled his hands. "I'm saying this simply as a friend to a friend. You needn't worry about your ranch."

"You mean the Judge didn't leave his half to his daughter?"

"No. He left it to his foster son. To you."

Shad swallowed hard. Harley Madison had truly been a father to him in the absence of his own. Now he realized he'd been considered more than just a ward.

"Abe needn't worry either," said Brent. "I'll leave the rest for the official reading of the will."

A thought occurred to Shad. "Is there any way that Hatten could know the contents of the will?"

"No. I'm sure he's merely assuming that, as the Judge's only blood relative, Anne will inherit everything, and the Judge is known to be rich."

"When do you have to disclose the contents?"

"Fairly soon," said Brent.

"Can you stall? Anne Madison's life might depend on it."

"Hatten sent a man in yesterday demanding that I read the Judge's will right away and turn over Miss Madison's inheritance."

No surprise.

"Well, do the best you can," said Shad. "I hate to ask this of you, but maybe you could close your office for a few days. Spend some time with your kids."

"If it turns out that I have to, I will," he promised. "Anyway, I'll take care of it. I noticed you came in the back way."

"Yes. I thought it best if no one saw me. I don't want anyone to know that I've talked to you."

"Good thinking. I'll tell Dooley to keep quiet about your visit. Now, you'd better get out of here before somebody comes in. I have an appointment in a few minutes."

They both stood and shook hands.

"Thanks," said Shad. "It's heartening to know that there're still some sane and sensible people in town."

With that, he slipped out of the lawyer's office by the same door he'd entered. After making sure that no one had seen him leave, he rode back to Abe's house. When he got there, the buggy was packed and hitched to a fine pair of horses. Lark sat straight-backed on the buggy seat, holding the reins. He had to admit that she was a fine-looking woman. From past experience he knew that she was strong and courageous as well. Abe climbed into the saddle and was ready to ride.

"Let's go," Lark said. "I'll feel a lot easier once we get to the ranch."

Because Abe's place was on the edge of town, they were able to slip away without attracting attention. On the ride back, Shad considered all that he'd learned. First of all, Hatten was a stock thief and a killer. No surprise there. Second, not everyone in town had bought into Hatten's trumped-up testimony. Good news. Third, the Judge had looked on him as a son and had left him the other half of his ranch. That touched him deeply. Last, Hatten was holding a prisoner who was most likely the Judge's daughter. He was going to have to act, and quickly. He couldn't let the Judge down. Especially not now.

Chapter Seven

Anne was instantly alert when she heard the bolt on her prison door lift. The door squeaked open, and Hatten stood framed in the entrance. A wave of fear washed over her. Was this where her life was going to end? She stood, smoothed her skirt, and faced him with all the calm and dignity she could muster.

"It's time to move you out," he said.

She stood frozen on the spot.

"Come on, gal!" he ordered. "If I have to drag you out of here, you're going to be mighty sorry."

She took a deep breath and placed one foot in front of the other. Her heart beat fast as she stepped into the sunlight.

"There's been too much snooping around," he said. "It wouldn't do for anyone to find you here."

She glanced at his face in an effort to read his intention. What she saw there was a mixture of slyness, greed, and contempt. There wasn't a spark of kindness or humanity to appeal to.

He grabbed her by one arm, propelling her along beside him.

"Where are you taking me?" she asked.

"That's none of your business."

How could it not be my business? she thought.

"If you kill me, they'll hunt you down like a rabid dog and hang you on the spot. You'll never get the chance to stand before a judge."

There was a short, harsh burst of laughter.

"Gal, they don't even know you're missing. Not even them Bolins up in Denver. Gert stepped into your shoes like they was made for her, and nobody's ever going to be looking for you."

A wave of hopelessness washed over her as she struggled to keep up.

"If you're so sure of that, why is there a need to move me? Why is there so much 'snooping around,' as you say? I saw a bunch of men out here demanding that I go back with them."

"Yeah. Gert came out and told 'em where to head in at. Looked and acted just like you. She was good. They won't be back."

Anne wondered, again, how anyone could mistake the coarse, older woman for herself.

Hatten shoved her onto the sagging porch of the ramshackle house, where the stench of garbage assaulted her nose. With his other hand he pushed open the door.

"Inside," he ordered.

Just then a rider came into view.

"It's that blasted Luke Crane," said Hatten. "Looks like he's got a bone to pick. Get on inside while I take care of him."

He gave Anne a shove, and she found herself in a room that was pasted floor to ceiling in old newspapers, no doubt for insulation. Those newspapers had absorbed dirt and cooking odors over time until they smelled almost as bad as the refuse pile. The room was filled with clutter and a few crude pieces of furniture. In the corners, masses of spiderwebs thrived undisturbed. She stepped around the debris that littered the floor. There was a room off to one side and another at the back. She could see into the one on the side. It contained a rumpled bed. Beside it, an old Indian woman was helping Gert to fix herself up. The blond woman glanced at Anne, then ignored her. Anne looked around for a weapon, but outside of a dirty pot with a broken handle, there was nothing.

Sounds of an argument came in from outside. She heard Hatten call for a couple of his men. Then there was silence.

It was only a matter of minutes before Hatten made his appearance. He looked toward the bedroom. "Will you stop primping, Gert?" he said. "I want you and the Ute to get some grub together."

"What for?" she asked, annoyed at the interruption.

"None of your business. Do as you're told."

That didn't set well with Gert, who came to the doorway. "Look here, Jed, you need me. You'd better start treating me right."

"Or what?" he challenged.

Gert was the one to back down. "I was just asking," she said.

"You need to pack some food because Hodge is coming to take the girl to the hideout."

They were talking about Anne as if she weren't there. But she saw the look of alarm that crossed Gert's face.

"Why do that?" Gert asked. "What's wrong with leaving her where she is?"

"I don't trust Featherstone. He's stubborn, and he's canny. I wouldn't put it past him to come back here and try another rescue. I'll rest a lot easier after she's gone."

Anne noticed that this story was different from the one he'd told her. It was clear that he was afraid of Abe Featherstone and his men. That gave her a glimmer of satisfaction if not hope. But the look she'd seen on Gert's face was ominous. Gert believed that Hatten was sending her away to be killed. No doubt the woman was right. She had to escape. The only thing to do was to wait and watch for her chance.

Hatten shoved a stool in her direction. "Sit down and be quiet," he ordered.

She did so. All the while she tried to think of a way out of her predicament.

A little later Gert came out of the kitchen and handed her a shawl. "You'll need this," she said almost kindly. "And this too. It's a package of cured ham and biscuits."

Anne took the things. "Thank you," she said, wondering if this was meant to become her last meal. The woman actually seemed sorry about what she believed was going to happen to Anne and was trying in her own way to be kind.

From outside came the sound of a horse approaching. Could it be Hodge, the man Hatten said was coming to take her away? Each moment was filled with dread as she waited for the rider to rein up in front of the shack.

"Come on," said Hatten, pulling her to her feet. "It's time for you to leave."

Anne draped the shawl around her shoulders and tied it. Then she went outside with him. The newcomer was waiting beside his horse. He was lean and sinewy with a face that vaguely reminded her of a vulture. He had another mount with him that was saddled and obviously meant for her.

"Here she is, Hodge," said Hatten. "You take good care of her, now."

To Anne, that command had an underlying meaning that chilled her to the bone.

Hodge took the food package she was holding and shoved it into one of his saddlebags. Then he took a piece of rawhide and bound her hands in front of her.

"Up you go," he said, and he boosted her into a saddle that was meant for a man. She'd ridden astride before, but not often. She grabbed hold of the reins. Much as she hated the place she was leaving, she dreaded what lay ahead even more.

Hodge kept a lead rope on her mare, so there was no chance of making a run for it. Even if she did, he'd probably just shoot her and be done with it. He carried a rifle in his saddle scabbard, and he wore a tied-down pistol like a gunfighter.

They rode west and slightly to the north. Once Anne glanced back at the shack. Gert was standing on the porch, watching.

Her captor rode without speaking. When the sun was directly overhead, he stopped.

"Time to rest for a spell," he said. He got down and came over to help her dismount.

She seated herself on the ground, and Hodge sat across from her. They ate the food Gert had sent and drank from a canteen. The horses nibbled on grass. She wanted to ask where he was taking her, but she was afraid of the answer. Since she couldn't run, maybe she could buy him off. Offer him money for her life.

"You may have heard that my father was a rich man," she said. "If you let me go, I'll see that you're well rewarded."

This got his attention. "Ma'am, the only reward your people would give me is a length of hemp swung over a cottonwood."

He went back to eating. Well, she thought, at least she'd tried.

When they were under way again, she thought of her father. She wished he were there. He'd know what to do. He always had an answer for everything. He'd even had one for her mother, when she told him that it was impossible to merge two such different lives. Well, merge them they had, though the union was unconventional to say the least. Anne had never known what it was like to have a normal family with two parents at home every day. Still, her mother was beautiful, talented, and independent. She had won lots of admirers in a town of more than five thousand people and many visitors. Unfortunately, a man with political ambitions couldn't have a wife who sang for drunken miners and other riffraff at a saloon, though Anne had been sheltered from that environment Now they were both dead. If she couldn't find a way to escape, she'd soon be joining them.

It was late when their journey came to an end. Anne was light-headed with fatigue. They'd stopped at the foot of a mesa, one of a number that thrust up here and there. Someone had built a crude shack against it that was almost invisible. It must be the hideout that Hatten had mentioned. Hodge helped her to dismount and then led her inside. It was so dark that the outlaw could scarcely find his way about. But at last he managed to light a candle.

"Over there," he said, pointing to one of the bunks that lined the back wall.

She went to it, stumbling once, and slid into the narrow bed.

"Go to sleep," said Hodge. "You're going to need your strength."

She gave him a look of alarm, for it occurred to her that he might shoot her while she slept.

He read her thoughts. "Don't worry, ma'am. I ain't never killed a woman, and I don't intend to start. But if I hadn't brung you away from there, Hatten would have got somebody else to do the job."

A flood of relief washed over her. The outlaw had a sense of honor.

"What will you tell your boss when you go back?" she asked.

"I ain't telling him nothing. Been meaning to go up to Wyoming for a long while. I reckon it's a good time to start."

"Thank you," she managed to say. "Thank you for my life."

With that she closed her eyes and slept.

It was dark when Shad and the Featherstones arrived back at the Judge's ranch house. The first order of business was to get Lark settled in. Then Shad took a lantern and made his way out to the bunkhouse. The men who weren't on watch were already bedded down. He spread his blanket roll on one of the empty bunks and crawled beneath the covers. It had been a long day, and he intended to go to sleep. He closed his eyes, but his mind was filled with questions.

Who was responsible for the Lazy M hands up and quitting like they did? It was their absence that had made the murder possible. With them gone, there were no witnesses and no one to interfere. Ponder was an old man, and he'd been easy to put out of action. The man behind this hadn't even tried to hire him away. No way was this a coincidence. And what had happened to loyalty, to riding for the brand? What inducement would it take to make those men abandon the Judge the way they had? Could it have been money alone? Whatever it was. Hatten was involved in it somehow.

Another thing that worried him was Tom Hobart's report about the prisoner in Hatten's shed. Who else could it be but the real Anne Madison? It pained him to think how close they'd been, only to have ridden off, not knowing she was there.

He considered the blond woman who'd taken Anne's place. She had nerve and bravado, but how did she think she could get away with her crude portrayal? That she and Hatten had been on familiar terms, he had no doubt. He was betting that Baca's inquiries would turn up information on her past—a woman like her had to have one.

It was late into the night when he finally slept.

Chapter Eight

A breakfast the next morning, Abe voiced his fears. "I don't know how much time that poor girl has left before that outlaw kills her. He's sure to get rid of her once he thinks that other woman has been accepted as Anne Madison."

Lark, who was busy filling their plates with flapjacks, turned. "What are you going to do, Abe?"

It was Shad who answered. "I've got a plan of sorts," he said. "It's the best I can come up with."

That got their attention.

"Look, we can't all go riding in there like we did before. Hatten will have his men on the alert, and they'll be ready to cut us down. On the other hand, one man might be able to do what a dozen can't."

"Meaning?" said Abe.

"Meaning that I'm going to slip in there after dark

and take Anne away. She'll be out of there before they suspect anything has happened." At least he hoped it would work that way.

Abe looked like he'd just swallowed a big spoonful of spring tonic. "I don't like it," he said. "You make it sound easy, but it ain't going to be. I promise you that."

Lark came over and put a hand on Shad's shoulder. "Look, we don't want to lose you and Anne both. There must be another way."

"If there is, I can't think of it. I know it's risky, but it has to be done. If I don't get her out of there, Hatten will kill her. He can't afford not to. We all know that. You also know how much I owe the Judge. I can't sit on my hands while they murder his daughter."

Abe sighed. "I understand," he said. "Maybe with a little luck you can pull this off. But you'd better bide your time until it's good and dark before you try to go in there."

Shad forked another bite before he answered. "That's my intention. I'll make like a phantom."

He tried to ignore the concerned looks Lark gave him as he finished the meal. Then he excused himself and went out to the barn. There was time to kill, and he needed to work off the restlessness he felt. He was in the midst of repairing some harness when Dobbs shouted that one of Baca's men was approaching. Shad laid his work aside and went out to meet the deputy from Trinidad.

"*Buenos días,* Moleres," he said as the deputy reined up. "What news do you bring?"

Moleres climbed down from the saddle. "Sheriff Baca received a reply about the woman," he said. "There is also word from the Bolins in Denver."

"Come on up to the house and have a cup of coffee. I know Abe is going to want to hear this too."

Abe welcomed the young deputy. "Good to see you," he said. "I believe you've met my wife."

Moleres gave a slight bow in Lark's direction. "*Buenos días, señora*," he said.

She returned the greeting.

"Been wondering if that boss of yours found out anything," said Abe. "Have a seat."

Lark brought him a cup of steaming hot coffee. Then they listened to what Moleres had to say.

"The lady in question is wanted in New Orleans for robbery. It seems she makes the acquaintance of wealthy gentlemen, then gets them intoxicated and robs them of their money and any jewelry they happen to be wearing. Her true name is Gertrude Bacon."

To Shad it seemed ironic that this was the kind of woman who'd captured the sympathy of some of the influential townspeople, even going so far as to demand his execution. Gertrude Bacon was a common thief. He wondered how those same townspeople would react when they learned about her identity and background. In fairness, many hadn't been fooled. But there were those who'd been quick to accept Hatten's testimony that he and Abe had hired a killer. They'd reined in Baca and his deputies, cutting off their help.

"What about the Bolins?" he asked.

"It seems they sent their ward to the stage station in the care of their hired man, an *hombre* called Chester Smith. Claimed they hadn't wanted to say good-bye in public. He came back and told them that she'd left on time for Trinidad. The following day, he quit without a word and disappeared. They thought it strange but said that Smith had always been a little odd. They're very upset about Miss Madison's disappearance, and they begged us to find her."

Shad thought the Bolins' excuse for not seeing Anne off themselves was a little lame. Had they done so, the kidnapping scheme would have failed. At least it would have been more difficult. He figured they'd be a whole lot more upset if they knew exactly how much danger they'd put Anne in. As far as he was concerned, they'd failed at the job they'd been hired to do.

"The sheriff regrets that he can't be of more help at this time," said Moleres, "but he intends to have Hernandez mention the contents of the first telegram to selected citizens. He believes this will change some minds."

"No matter," said Shad. "I intend to take care of this myself."

The deputy gave him a questioning look. "Señor Wakefield, that doesn't tell me very much."

"Then how about this? We have reason to believe that Anne Madison is being held prisoner in a shed on Hatten's ranch. I'm going up there to try to free her. It's the only way without a bloodbath. I'll wait until dark, slip in, and get her out."

Moleres looked thoughtful. "You're probably right about its being the only way. But you have to get in there and get out without being caught. That may not be so easy."

"Well, I'll do my best."

The deputy looked at him with respect. "Then I wish you luck. You're going to need it."

"If anybody can pull this off, Shad can," said Abe. "We're obliged to you for bringing word from the sheriff."

"De nada," he said. "It is nothing. Sheriff Baca regrets that he can't do more at the moment."

After Moleres had left, Shad went back to the bunkhouse to clean and load his guns. As an afterthought he slipped a knife into his belt. Then he went to the corral to get Squire and to select a spare mount to take along for Anne to ride. The horse that he chose for her was black, a color that would be hard to spot at night. He saddled them both, taking care to tighten the cinches. Then he packed his saddlebags, making sure to include plenty of ammunition. After a quick stop at the house for food, he'd be ready to pull out. Lark had a plate of beans and cornbread waiting for him. While he ate, she packed a generous amount of jerked beef and biscuits.

"You'll need to keep up your strength," she said. "No doubt that poor girl will need nourishment too."

Lark was expressing faith in his ability to do the job. He hoped he wouldn't disappoint her.

Abe was waiting for him at the corral. He had a serious look on his face. "You be careful, son," he warned. "I want you and that girl back here unharmed."

"I'll do my best," he promised.

Shad threw his leg over the saddle and headed Squire north. The black followed on a lead rope. As he rode, he tried not to think of the trouble that lay ahead. Instead, he concentrated on the land around him. It was the land where he'd been born and bred. Some said that Colorado was on the brink of statehood. It would happen soon, he believed. Perhaps in a few years. Maybe more. But it was bound to happen. The Transcontinental Rail Road had recently been completed, and more and more rail roads were connecting the West to the East. The Santa Fe Trail, which had created the town of Trinidad, would soon become a page in a history book as rail commerce took its place. Anyone could tell that the Territory was ripe for that final step into statehood. No doubt the Judge would have been an important figure during and after that transition. Anyway, that had been his intention, and he'd been an astute politician.

Shad considered the cost of his mentor's political ambitions. The secrecy the Judge had deemed necessary in order to protect his reputation had separated him from his wife and daughter. Much as he respected Harley Madison, it was his own opinion that family should come first. He felt sorry for the daughter who was kept under wraps all those years. He knew for a fact that a number of well-to-do matrons in the West had much more scandalous beginnings than Rowena

Madison, who'd done nothing worse than sing in a saloon. But even after Rowena's death, a daughter would have raised questions, and the Judge's past relationship would have been scrutinized with disfavor.

As for men, Shad knew of some political figures who'd divorced their wives of long-standing in favor of much younger, prettier women. To him that was far worse than falling in love with a saloon singer. No doubt after the initial scandal, the electorate might well have been more tolerant than the Judge had expected.

Shad rode slowly, letting the day grow late. It was near dusk when he came within sight of the Hatten place. He rode into a draw to hide and rest the horses until it was fully dark. Thankfully the bright harvest moon was still nights away. That was a piece of luck; for tonight he needed the cover of darkness.

"You know we've got to get her out of there," he said to Squire when it came time to leave. "I'm counting on you."

He stepped into the stirrup and rode out of the draw with the black horse still on the rope. In the distance he could see a tiny bobbing light. Someone was on his way to the barn. Light also spilled from the cracks in the shutters of the house and the bunkhouse.

He recalled Tom Hobart's description of the shed where they were keeping the prisoner, and he remembered seeing it himself when he was there. It was off by itself, away from the other buildings. Its isolation would serve to make his task a little easier.

He rode in as close as he dared. Then he swung down

from the saddle and led the horses. A cloud scudded across the face of the quarter moon, cloaking its scant light. Slowly he moved forward before stopping and ground-tethering Squire and the black. Quickly he replaced his boots with soft-soled moccasins. This was a time for stealth. He would go the rest of the way on foot. The .44 was a comforting weight at his side. He checked to see that the knife was secure in his belt. A cold wind stung his face as he slipped across the open space like a ghost.

He'd covered a couple dozen yards before he heard the sound of a raucous argument coming from the bunkhouse to his right. A poker game was in full swing. He paused a minute to see if anyone was going to be thrown out. When that didn't happen, he continued. The cloud cover that had obscured the moon passed on, leaving the shed in plain view. Dropping into a crouch, he ran toward it.

The sight of a cigarette being lit caused him to freeze. A guard was standing in the shadow of the shed, watching the bunkhouse. The match was extinguished, leaving the lit cigarette tip for anyone to see.

Before Shad could move on, the door of the house, which lay to the south of the bunkhouse, banged open, and Hatten appeared, backlit, on the porch.

"Avery, get your backside over here!" he yelled. "I want to talk to you."

This caused an even bigger commotion in the bunkhouse. Shad heard a piece of furniture smack the floor. His hand instinctively went to his revolver.

Avery came to the bunkhouse doorway. "What is it you want?" he called.

"Don't stand there and question me, you little whelp," said Hatten. "Do as you're told."

Avery had some choice things to say, but his uncle had already gone back into the house and slammed the door. As Shad watched, Avery grudgingly crossed the distance. He was obeying Hatten's orders, but it was clear that he didn't like it. From the bunkhouse came sounds of the game resuming without him.

Silently Shad circled around to come up behind the guard. The man was enjoying his smoke, and he'd been distracted by the set-to between Hatten and his nephew. All this was in Shad's favor. With one swift move he pinned the outlaw with his left arm, and with his right hand he held the knife to his throat. The outlaw dropped the remains of his smoke and grabbed for Shad's arms.

"Hold still and don't make a sound if you want to live," Shad warned, his voice barely above a whisper.

The guard ceased to struggle.

"Now, you're going to lift the bar on that door. Easy-like."

The outlaw reached out and lifted the bar, then let it slip to the ground.

"Now pull the door open."

It was even darker inside the shed than it was outside.

"Anne," he called softly, "I'm a friend of your father's. I've come to take you away from here."

"I surely do appreciate the rescue," came a masculine voice from the back of the prison, "even though my name's not Anne."

That took Shad by surprise. He almost dropped the knife. A large man stepped through the opening.

"What happened to Anne Madison?" he asked the guard.

"I swear I don't know," he said, his voice a raspy whisper.

Shad didn't believe him. He pressed the blade tighter. "Tell me, and be quick about it."

The outlaw made a gurgling noise, and Shad eased the pressure.

"The boss came and took her away," he gasped. "I don't know what he done with her after that. She wasn't gone long before he threw Crane in here."

Crane? He'd thought that voice sounded familiar. He was freeing the man who'd tried to hang him a few years back when he worked for him on the Circle C.

From the bunkhouse came the sound of scraping chairs, a sign that the poker game was breaking up. The door opened, and one of the men came out and shouted Avery's name. Any sound from Crane or the guard, and Shad was done for. He waited, scarcely daring to breathe. Seconds passed. Finally, after getting no answer, the man gave up and went back inside.

"We've got to get out of here," said Crane.

Before he realized what Crane was about to do, his former boss grabbed the guard's gun from its holster and knocked the outlaw unconscious with the butt of his own pistol.

"Now, where's your horses?" he demanded.

"This way," said Shad. "But for Pete's sake be quiet."

They'd almost made it when Crane caught his boot in a gopher hole. He fell, swearing as he hit the ground. That was enough to rouse the hands in the bunkhouse.

"Somebody's out there!" one of them yelled. "Come on! Let's get 'em!"

Shad lit out running. So did Crane, whose survival instincts finally clicked in.

"They're getting away!" came the outcry. "Hurry!"

They spurred their horses just as the outlaws began firing. It would take time for Hatten and his men to saddle their mounts and give chase, and every minute took them farther away from the stronghold. Besides, the darkness was their ally.

They were miles away when it was clear they weren't being pursued. Shad slowed the dun to a walk.

"I'm obliged to you, whoever you are," said Luke Crane.

It was too dark for Crane to see, and he didn't recognize Shad's voice. When Shad thought of what the older man had tried to do to him, he had to fight back his rage. Crane, always a hothead, had accused him of murdering his own partner. Then he'd tried to hunt him down and lynch him. Even after Shad was cleared of the murder, Crane refused to accept that he'd made a mistake.

"I'm surprised you don't remember me," said Shad.

"Should I?"

"I reckon. I'm your worst enemy."

"No. Whoever you are, you're not that. My worst enemy is Jed Hatten."

"Then we've finally got something in common."

"Do I know you?" Crane asked, squinting at Shad in the moonlight.

"You ought to. I gave you a beating when you tried to lynch me for a killing I didn't do."

The man swore. "Shad Wakefield. Who'd have thought?"

Certainly not Shad. His former boss had been nothing but a bitter memory to him, and he'd planned to keep it that way.

When they stopped to give the horses a breather, Shad asked what Crane knew about the woman who'd been a prisoner in the shed.

"I didn't see anyone. There's a woman in the house, of course, but she's not a prisoner. She's with Hatten."

While he didn't like Luke Crane and didn't trust him, he believed he was telling the truth.

"How long were you in there?"

"Since this morning."

"What's Hatten got against you, anyway?"

There was a pause. Crane seemed reluctant to answer.

"It's something I found out and confronted him with," he said at last. I don't like being used. Hatten used me."

Shad waited, but there was no further explanation. It was a strange turn of events that had made the man an ally. At least for the time being. But he wasn't about to forget that his former enemy was armed with the out-law's gun. Neither would he forget how Crane had turned against him, demanding his life. A close call with a noose was something a fellow didn't take light-ly, nor did he soon forget. He didn't think Crane had forgotten his humiliation at Shad's hands either, or the embarrassment of being wrong. Nonetheless, he couldn't leave the man without a horse, and he dang sure wasn't going to give him the Judge's horse. There was nothing to do but bring him along. They mounted up again.

Another mile passed before Crane decided to explain what he'd been talking about. "I'm not proud of how I let Hatten use me," he said.

Shad didn't comment. There was a lot that Crane couldn't be proud of.

"You've no doubt wondered why all Judge Madison's hands quit him."

"I heard that somebody hired them away for better wages," said Shad.

"A whole lot better wages. That fellow was me."

Shad reined up, and his hand went to the grips of his .44.

"You mean you've got the nerve to confess to being in on the Judge's murder?"

"No, no," said Crane. "Not knowingly, anyway. I didn't know what Hatten was up to. I swear."

"Then tell me, just how much does it take to buy a man's loyalty?"

"I'm paying 'em double. Guess you're wondering

why I'd do something like that. Well, after that little misunderstanding we had awhile back, nobody who was any good wanted to work for me anymore. All I could get was a few ne'er-do-wells who'd come wandering in, work for awhile, and then pull up stakes. I figured it was all your fault. Yours and the Judge's. After all, he'd talked me into hiring you in the first place."

The lie about the Judge angered Shad even more. "The Judge didn't have anything to do with that, Crane, and you know it. In fact, he tried to get me to stay on with him."

"Do tell? The truth of it is, Wakefield, he told me to hire you because you needed to be seasoned a bit. Said you ought to be off on your own for awhile until you got some age and experience. Well, I did what he said and hired you. It ended up practically ruining me."

Shad's anger was diverted to the Judge. He'd manipulated him into doing exactly what he wanted. In short, Harley Madison had treated him like a dumb kid. Still, the way he saw it, Crane's troubles had nothing to do with the Judge. It was Crane who was the hothead. It was Crane who'd betrayed and hunted down his own man for a lynch rope. He'd made himself look like a fool and sealed his reputation. His men left him, and good men refused to work for him.

"You should have known that I wouldn't shoot my partner, Charlie," he said. "You wouldn't even listen to my side."

"I might have been a little hasty," Crane admitted. "But

if you're interested, Hatten used to work for me. He was one of those ne'er-do-wells that I mentioned. He heard the story about what happened between you and me. Later, it was Hatten who pointed out that I was short on hands, and he knew where I could get some good ones if I'd be willing to pay double for awhile. At the same time I could get back at the Judge and leave him high and dry. He'd started rumors among the Judge's hands, undermining their respect for him, and by the time I made my offer, I was able to hire every last one of 'em away, except for that old man. Didn't even bother to try for him."

Shad struggled to hold his temper. "None of them had worked for Madison long, or they'd have known him better. What's more, they wouldn't have trusted those double wages to last if they'd known you better."

"Could be," Crane admitted. "Anyway, I didn't know Hatten was setting the Judge up to be shot. When I figured it out, I was mad that he'd used me. I rode down here to confront him. Guess I should have brought some backup, 'cause he had a couple of his men lock me in that shed."

"The way I see it," said Shad, "you're luckier than you deserve. It's a wonder Hatten didn't shoot you right away."

"Might have, except I told him my men would go to the sheriff with my story if I failed to show up. I think he was planning to pay me off once I'd cooled down."

"Sounds like all he could do," Shad agreed. "Then I came along and upset the buggy. I think Sheriff Baca's going to want to hear your story."

"Wouldn't be surprised. I just hope that poor girl is still alive."

Crane wasn't the only one.

The sun was up by the time they got back to the Lazy M. Abe was at the corral, and he looked surprised to see Luke Crane riding in with Shad.

"Well, Shadrach," he said. "I was expecting you to come back with somebody a whole sight prettier than this *hombre.*"

Crane's narrow-set eyes, beak nose, and wide shoulders were a far cry from the young girl Abe had hoped to see.

"I was too late," Shad confessed. "They'd already moved her. Crane, here, was her replacement."

Toby appeared. "I'll take care of the horses," he said.

"Obliged," said Shad. "Rub 'em both down and give 'em a bait of oats. They've earned it."

Crane appeared awkward and uncertain of his welcome. "Look," he said, "I'm sorry as can be that you weren't able to rescue that girl. Still, I'm glad to be free."

Abe didn't look on Crane as a friend, but he invited him to the house for breakfast. "I'm interested in how you got crosswise of Hatten," he said.

"I can tell you right now that it was cussed stupidity on my part. But I guess you're going to want to hear all of it."

When they got to the house and Crane was introduced to Lark, she couldn't hide her surprise, for she'd been told about the man. Tactfully she pretended she hadn't and set about making flapjacks.

At the table, Crane told his story to the Featherstones and Toby. Also to Kershaw, who'd come to join them.

"I'm not proud of what I done to the Judge," he concluded. "Not proud at all. I want to get his killer as bad as any of you."

"But where do you suppose they've taken Anne?" said Lark, her concern apparent in her voice.

That was the question on all their minds.

Shad turned to Toby. "We need you to ride into town again. Tell Sheriff Baca everything you've just heard. Warn him to be careful if he runs into any of Hatten's men. If they come to town, he'd do well to arrest them. There's a lot of this we know for sure now."

Toby pushed back his chair and got up. "I'll leave right away. But, Shad, what are you going to do?"

"We're going back."

"What if you're too late?" said Lark.

Shad hesitated before he answered. "Just pray that we're not."

"You look dead on your feet, son," said Abe. "Before you head out or do anything, you've got to get some shut-eye."

"But when you're ready to ride, I'm going with you," said Kershaw with newfound courage. "I've got a score to settle too."

"Then let me have an hour's sleep, and I'll be ready," said Shad.

"Think I'll catch a nap myself," said Crane. "It was a long night."

Leaving it to Abe to make the preparations, Shad escorted his old enemy to the bunkhouse.

"Take your pick," he said of the vacant bunks.

Crane chose one, and Shad took another for himself. Immediately he fell asleep.

Chapter Nine

Shad had rolled out of his bunk and tried to recall why he was sleeping in broad daylight. Then he remembered his night ride and his failure to rescue Anne. Loud snores from the other side of the room reminded him that by a strange quirk of fate he'd become allied with his former enemy, Luke Crane. But he'd failed to find Anne, so now he had to go back and finish what he'd started. He pulled on his boots, belted on his pistol, and went outside.

McNary was waiting for him at the corral. "Abe just told me what happened," said the foreman. "Looks like we've got a job to do."

Grim-faced, Shad nodded. He didn't like the idea of leading his men into a shoot-out with Hatten's outlaws, but that's what it had come down to.

Crane emerged from the bunkhouse and joined them.

131

"Well, well, look what the coyotes drug in," said McNary, who was no admirer of Shad's former boss.

"You can keep your gun holstered," said Crane. "This time I'm on your side."

The look McNary gave him was doubtful. It was plain that he wasn't sure having Crane on his side was a good thing. "The men are eager to get started," he said.

Dobbs, Montoya, Rutledge, and Lemke had congregated by the barn, their mounts saddled and waiting. Abe and McNary made six. Crane, seven. Eight in all. How many would come back?

"We're leaving Kershaw and Ponder here to wait for Toby," said McNary.

Shad agreed with the plan.

Abe approached them, leading the California sorrel that had belonged to the Judge. He pointedly ignored Crane. "Squire needs a rest," he said. "Ride McBeth, here. He's strong and fast with a lot of staying power."

Shad grabbed the reins and mounted up. They headed out once more for the Hatten ranch. A few hours' sleep had made a big difference. Shad felt renewed. His only regret was losing that time. With seven guns to back him up, he'd make the outlaw tell what he'd done with the real Anne Madison, and for Hatten's sake, she'd better be alive and well.

At the same time Shad was heading north, Anne was heading south on a parallel course. The sun was well above the horizon as Anne sweet-talked the mare, urging her forward. The grassy plains stretched out before her, seemingly to the edge of the world. She felt an almost overwhelming sense of relief and gratitude at having been spared a terrible death. But she realized the danger was far from over. And not just from Hatten's outlaws. A while back news of a Cheyenne raid on a stage station had reached Denver, and no one knew if there might be others. Still, the threat from the Cheyenne was remote. The one from Hatten was imminent. When Hodge failed to return, he'd certainly come looking for her. The farther away from the mesa hideout she could get, the better. The memory of looking into the outlaw's cold, soulless eyes made her shudder. She couldn't let him get his hands on her again.

Her thoughts turned to Aunt Sadie and Uncle Art up in Denver. No doubt they believed her to be safe and sound at her father's ranch, among her father's friends. But if Hatten succeeded in killing her, what would happen when they came to visit? The outlaw would have to get rid of them too, for they'd expose the imposter who'd taken her place. She had to survive. Not only for herself, but for her foster parents as well.

When it came time to give the mare a breather, she dismounted and checked the saddlebags the outlaw had sent with her. To her surprise she discovered a Colt pistol and a supply of ammunition. She knew how to handle a gun. Her father had taught her. She blessed Hodge for giving her this weapon against trouble. Outlaw though he was, in his own way he was a gentleman.

Over in the west great thunderheads were piling up.

The afternoon would surely bring rain, and she had nothing for protection but the shawl Gert had given her. Searching the other saddlebag, she found a waterproof poncho and said another silent thank-you. The poncho was the dull color of slate, making it hard to spot from a distance. She shook it out and slipped it on.

Every so often she paused to look over her trail, dreading what she might see. As the hours passed, the thunderheads became more ominous. She needed to make haste, but she also needed to find shelter. There was nothing close, but in the distance another mesa rose from the plain. There, she might be able to find an overhang or outcrop that would offer a measure of protection from the storm. While lightning was known for its wild, frightening displays on mountaintops, she knew it could strike death on the flatland as well.

Distances on the open plains were much greater than they appeared, she knew. Before she reached the mesa, the storm had moved in close. She could smell the moisture in the air. To the west a jagged streak of lightning forked across a cloud. Thunder rumbled.

"Come on, girl," she urged the mare. "We've got to hurry."

Just as she was approaching the base of the mesa, the sky opened up, and it began to pour. Through the thick curtain of falling water, she spotted a wind-eroded cave. The climb to the shelter was short, but it was difficult due to the rain-slick ground. The mare slid more than once and had to struggle to keep her footing.

At the cave entrance Anne dismounted and led the mare inside. There, she pulled off the saddle and wiped the horse down with a rag from one of the saddlebags.

"Good girl," she crooned softly. "I'm proud of you."

A sudden flash of lightning startled the animal. Anne kept tight hold of the mare's reins as a thunderbolt followed the light.

"Steady there," she said. "Nothing's going to hurt you."

At the sound of her voice and the reassuring touch of her hand, the mare calmed down.

One of her father's stories popped into her head. She was a little girl on his knee when he told her that thunder was really a party of giants in the sky who were lawn bowling. Thoughts of him were always bittersweet, accompanied by a painful feeling of loss. Still, in a strange way they were comforting too.

The poncho had protected her well, but the shelter itself was cold and damp. She fished out matches and tinder from the supplies she'd been given. Then, after gathering small branches and twigs that had blown up against the back wall, she started a fire. When this was done, she propped up a flat rock to serve as a reflector. Soon the small cave was warm, almost cozy, while outside the deluge continued.

A feeling of weariness swept over her. Fear and flight had drained her strength. After looking north through the rainfall and seeing no riders, she took the bedroll that had been fastened behind the cantle and made a pallet on the cave floor. The fire warmed and comforted her, and she fell asleep.

Shad and his small band of followers weren't far from Hatten's stronghold when all around them a stillness blanketed the land like the calm before a storm.

"I don't like the looks of it," said Abe, pointing to the sky. "The way them clouds are building up, we're apt to have a gully washer."

Shad, too, had been eyeing the build-up of storm clouds. It was a little late in the year for rain, but from time to time it happened.

McNary rode up beside him. "I don't like what's coming," he said. "One time when I was herding cattle, I saw a lightning bolt hit a man. It wasn't a pretty sight."

Shad had been on the range during storms more times than he cared to remember. He didn't like being exposed to lightning either. They were a little to the southwest of Hatten's place when the storm broke.

"This might be a good thing," said Abe. "Them outlaws will be holed up, and they won't be expecting us. What's more, if any of that scum has harmed Anne, I'm going to make 'em think it's raining fire and brimstone."

An Old Testament retribution, thought Shad. Abe could dispense the modern version of it with fists or guns. And he'd have a lot of help.

When they were close enough to see the shack and the other buildings, he gave the order to spread out. "We'll ride in fast and be on top of 'em before they know we're here." At least that's what he hoped.

He kicked the sorrel in the sides and galloped out in front of the others. But instead of the expected gunfire, they were met with silence. The place appeared to be deserted.

McNary rode to the corral and then looked inside the barn. "Hey, all the horses are gone. Hatten's pulled out."

"Wait here," said Shad. "I'm going to have a look inside the house."

He climbed down and stepped onto the rickety porch. When he gave the door a shove, it swung open. His nose was assaulted with the stench of old food odors, mustiness, and dirt. With his gun drawn, he looked into all three rooms. They were empty.

"Search everything," he ordered as he stepped back outside. "They may have left her here somewhere, dead or alive."

They started looking. Just in case, Shad headed over to the outbuilding where Crane had been imprisoned, though he didn't expect to find that they'd brought Anne back. The bolt was still lying in the dirt, and the door was ajar as he'd left it.

"Find any tracks?" he asked as he rejoined the others.

"The rain's done a good job of washing them out," said Crane. "But there's some over on the lee side of the barn."

Shad went and took a look. Instead of going north toward Crane's ranch as he would have guessed, they were headed west.

"How about we wait inside the barn until the downpour stops?" said Dobbs. "The storm can't last too much longer."

Shad glanced around at the men who'd accompanied him. They were wet and bedraggled in spite of their ponchos. No doubt they were cold as well.

"Good idea," he agreed. "The horses could use a rest, and maybe we can dry off a little."

He was surprised to find that the inside of the barn was a lot cleaner than the house. They dried off the horses and fed them from a supply of oats that had been left behind. They had to forego a fire and hot coffee, for the inside of a barn was way too combustible.

"Where do you suppose they went?" said Abe.

That was the question on all their minds. "Wish I knew," said Shad.

"You've got 'em worried," said McNary. "Hatten was counting on his scheme going off like he'd pictured it in his head. But it hasn't done that. Things started going wrong almost from the start."

Would that cause him to abandon his plan altogether and make a run for it? Or would he try to brazen his way through? What would the Judge do if he were here and in charge of this unofficial posse?

Shad thought about it for awhile. Most likely Harley Madison would give Abe's threat of fire and brimstone a new and more terrifying meaning as he rained it down on Hatten and everyone else connected with the outlaw's vicious scheme.

The downpour stopped as suddenly as it had begun.

Overhead, the moisture-gorged clouds were moving on to pour their abundance onto the thirsty plains to the east.

"Let's get ready to ride," said Shad.

They were soon following the most direct course to the west, the way that was indicated by what tracks they could find. A few miles from the barn the outlaws' trail intercepted those of two other riders. One of them was much heavier than his companion. Abe, who was a pretty fair tracker, perked up at the sight.

"That one set might belong to a woman," he said. "Maybe to Anne."

Neither Shad nor any of the others wanted to remind him that there were two other women, Gertie Bacon and the Ute housekeeper, in Hatten's group. Still, the tracks offered hope.

From that point on the two appeared to be followed by the gang. Shad wondered why they'd started out ahead of the others. *Was it possible that someone had helped Anne escape?*

It was dusk when they arrived at the base of a mesa and discovered a partially hidden shack.

Shad climbed down from the sorrel and took a look around. "Looks like the gang divided here," he said. "It appears that most of 'em rode north. But four riders headed south."

There were other signs as well. Two horses had spent the night in the lean-to attached to the shack. One of them carried its rider north. The other carried a light-weight rider, probably a woman, southward.

"I think Anne's still alive," he said. "Somebody got her away. Then the others came after her."

"Could be," said McNary. "I think the man who was with her went north to draw Hatten and the rest of 'em off her."

"If he did, it didn't work," said Shad. "Looks like four of the gang rode south."

"Well, it's getting too dark to follow their tracks," said Crane. "If you ask me, we'd be better off waiting until first light.

"I expect he's right," said McNary. "Hatten won't be able to track Anne at night either. He'll have to hold off."

Shad could tell that Abe didn't like having to wait. Fact was, he wasn't too happy about it himself. Still, what Crane and McNary said made sense. They'd be better off staying at the hideout, letting the horses rest, and getting a good night's sleep.

He made the decision. "We'll ride at dawn," he said.

They were to take turns standing watch in case the outlaws decided to return. As they were bedding down, Shad asked Abe a question that had been puzzling him. "How were you planning to tell if that woman was the real Anne Madison?"

There was a pause before his old friend answered. "I was wondering how long it'd take you to get around to asking," he said. "Well, I'll tell you. According to the Judge, that girl's got a voice just like her mother's. Even when she was a small child, she used to sing him

making trouble. It didn't help that Gert was less than convincing either. Now, because of Hodge's treachery, the Madison girl might well get to Trinidad and start wagging her tongue. Not to mention the trouble Crane could cause if he started blabbing. It was enough to make a man despair. He was surrounded by incompetents and traitors.

Things had been different back in the Missouri hill country during the war. There hadn't been any law to speak of. Most of the able-bodied men were gone, and he and his partners had free rein. It had been easy for them to ride up to a farmhouse and do as they pleased. He had relished the feeling of power it gave him to see the frightened faces of those groveling farm families. But the war had ended, vigilante groups had sprung up like mushrooms, and the Ozarks got downright unhealthy. Dade and Glausser were shot. Smitty was hanged. The rest, like himself, took off for friendlier climes. Colorado Territory had given them a second chance. But unless he could turn things around, he was going to need a third.

"It's too dark to go on," said Avery. "We ought to stop and make camp. That draw over there looks like a good place."

Hatten was quick to agree with his nephew, for he was bone weary. The shallow draw had already drained and dried, and it offered a measure of protection from the chill October night. Avery busied himself making a fire from sticks and tinder brought from the ranch. When it blazed to life, they shared a meal and warmed themselves beside the flames.

Hatten bedded down soon after, taking care to keep his pistol close at hand beneath the blankets. Gert wasn't to be trusted. Not that he fully trusted anyone. But he was paying the gunman, Corby Bray, a good deal of money. And as for Avery, he knew where his own best chances lay. Gert was another matter. She'd failed in their mission and was becoming a liability. It looked like he'd have to get rid of her, and it was possible that she sensed this. Women were peculiar that way. They sometimes knew things they had no way in the world of knowing.

Off in the distance a coyote howled at the moon. It was a lonesome sound. He knew that some might take it for an omen. A bad one.

He was still seething over Hodge's betrayal. Not only had it caused him a ton of trouble, it was also setting a bad example for the rest. It had given him no small measure of satisfaction to order the men he'd sent after Hodge to shoot him on sight.

Through slitted eyes he watched Gert stand and stretch in the firelight. She was a fine figure of a woman, he had to admit. For an instant he regretted her death sentence. But the moment quickly passed. Her days were numbered.

"Look, I don't know why you had to drag me along," she complained, sensing his interest. "I could have stayed back at the hideout and waited. It's bad enough that I get caught in a storm. Now I have to ride all day and sleep on the ground to boot."

"You'll do whatever I tell you," he said. "What's more, you'll keep your mouth shut about it."

He could see her face in the firelight. She looked as if she'd just been slapped.

"Maybe I shouldn't bring it up," said Avery from his bed on the other side of the camp, "but it looks to me like we're in a lot of trouble."

"Figured that out by yourself, did you?"

His tone served as a warning. Neither Avery nor Bray said another word.

"All of you listen to me," said Hatten after a long silence. "Up ahead somewhere we've got us a ticket to riches. Once we get our hands on that Madison girl, we'll hold her hostage and demand whatever we want."

"What about me?" said Gert. "I'm your ticket to riches. I'm going to collect that pompous old coot's estate."

"You messed it up," said Hatten, his voice cold. "I gave you a simple little acting part, and you went and messed it up."

"I can still pull this off," she protested. "All you have to do is catch that girl before anyone sees her, and we can all go on just like before."

Hatten wished that were so. If things had worked out like he'd pictured, he'd be days away from being one of the richest men in Colorado.

As if reading his thoughts, Bray spoke up. "It's too late, Gert," he said "They caught on to what the boss was doing before he had a chance to pull it off."

Hatten's anger flared. It pained him to have his fail-ure pointed out that way, especially by an inferior. He balled his fists and started to lash out at the gunman. Just in time he remembered how many men Bray had killed.

"You're right," he said, struggling to keep the emo-tion from his voice. "I didn't have enough time to get the job done. But now the situation has changed. We're going to capture that Madison girl and make 'em pay for her release."

"She's more'n likely halfway to Trinidad by now," said Avery.

"We'll get her. Don't worry. Now shut up and let me get some sleep."

He settled back and closed his eyes. The night around him was still except for the whispers of the wind across the grassland and the mournful sound of that lone coyote.

Again he considered how his plan had gotten off track. As he saw it, Wakefield was largely to blame. After the Judge's body was discovered, Wakefield should have been half mad for vengeance. According to plan, he was to follow Kershaw's clearly marked trail and shoot it out with him. Since Kershaw had just enough cartridges to start something, Wakefield had an overwhelming advantage. With the Judge's "killer" dead—case closed. Who'd have thought Wakefield would let him live? If only a single bullet had found its mark, everything would have turned out differently. Gert would be filling the Madison girl's place, no matter how poorly. Then, after she'd become his bride, Gert would eventually have made him a rich widower. On that thought, he fell asleep.

He couldn't say how much time had passed when he woke with a start. His hand went to the revolver beside him. Could someone be out there in the darkness? Was that what had disturbed his sleep? He lay quietly listening. A minute passed. Then two. The fire had burned itself out, and all he heard were the sounds of snoring. Reassured, he relaxed. Of late he was getting way too jumpy. He closed his eyes and drifted off to sleep again.

Night riding had brought Shad far from the mesa hideout. Now, at daybreak, fog covered the land and obscured the sun. He wasn't sure when it happened, but somewhere during the night he must have bypassed the outlaws' camp, even though he hadn't spotted a campfire, nor had he seen or heard anything that would give them away.

The sorrel was worth whatever the Judge had paid for him. With no more consideration than a brief rest from time to time, McBeth was holding his own.

An hour passed, maybe more, before the sun burned off the fog, enabling him to see a tabletop mountain up ahead. He tried to put himself in Anne's place and think as she would have thought. When that storm caught her out in the open, she would have looked for shelter. If she'd left Hatten's hideout at dawn, as he believed, she would have been near that mesa. Maybe he could find where she'd sheltered. Having been wet, cold, and tired, maybe she was still there.

As he drew closer, he spotted a cave. It was high enough to provide a good vantage point.

"Come on, McBeth," he said. "I'm betting that's the place we're looking for."

He closed the distance, and McBeth picked his way up the slope.

"Hold it right there!" The voice came from within the cave, and it belonged to a woman.

When next Hatten awoke, a pale, diffuse light was creeping over the horizon. The others were still asleep. He threw his blankets off and looked over the fog-shrouded plains. Everything was obscured by the dense covering. He wondered if they were closing in on the Madison girl. There were signs that she'd spent the night before last at the mesa hideout. No doubt she'd left early yesterday.

The fog was a problem, but it would lift soon. When it was gone, there would still be visual impediments. The land wasn't level. There were washes, dips in the landscape, mesas, and hills. Still, Hatten prided himself on being something of a tracker. Wherever she went, he would follow.

"Avery, get your lazy backside up, and get that fire going," he ordered, nudging his nephew hard with the toe of one boot.

Avery came out of his bedroll as if a rattlesnake had crawled into it. Bray didn't have to be told. Neither did

Gert. She got up looking as bedraggled as a horse that had been rode hard and put away wet. He wondered how he'd ever thought she was pretty. Already lines had formed around her mouth and eyes. Her color was sallow, and her hair hung limp and dirty. There was no way this common saloon girl and petty thief could pass for a high-toned Judge's daughter, at least not the way she looked and acted now.

"Hurry up with that fire," he said. "We gotta ride."

From somewhere in his pack Avery was able to come up with bits of tinder and a few more sticks of wood. Hatten, meanwhile, gathered up his bedroll and ground cloth. He noticed that Gert was uncommonly quiet, but that was a welcome change. He was good and tired of her whining and nagging.

After a hurried meal they saddled their horses and rode out of the draw. A lot depended on what happened today. It might well decide whether he'd become a rich man or end up dead. He fully intended to end up rich.

It appeared that Shad had found what he was looking for. "Anne Madison?" he said.

"Yes, and you can ride on back and tell Hatten that his game is over. I've got friends."

"Yes, and I'm one of them. My name is Shad Wakefield. You may have heard your father speak of me."

There was a pause. "Get off your horse and walk this way. I want to get a good look at you. And don't try anything."

Shad did as he was told.

"That's far enough," she warned.

While he stood there waiting with the reins of the sorrel in his left hand, she stepped into the open. In spite of her ordeal, she was beautiful. She bore only a superficial resemblance to the woman who was impersonating her. All they had in common was hair the color of wheat and sky-blue eyes. In her right hand she held a pistol, and it was aimed directly at his belly. Anne Madison wasn't bluffing.

He imagined how he must look to her, scruffy and trail-worn as he was. No different from the outlaws, probably.

"How do I know you're who you say you are?" she asked, a quaver in her voice that she couldn't control.

Good question. The answer came to him from out of nowhere.

"I hear that you and your father are partial to the tune 'Annie Laurie,' " he said.

She lowered the gun. "No one but a friend would know that. I'm very glad to meet you at last, Shad Wakefield."

"Guess you've had a bad time of it, and it isn't over yet. Hatten and three others are still out there, and they're headed this way."

She gazed out over the plains, trying to spot them. "I'm not surprised," she said. "You'd better come on inside the cave. We can ford up there. Bring your horse. There's room.

"Not a good idea," he said. "It was a fine shelter from the storm and through the night, but if Hatten's outfit starts shooting, it'll be a death trap. Bullets bouncing off the walls can make mincemeat out of human flesh."

"I see," she said. "We can't let them take us."

"No, ma'am. You're right about that. What we're going to have to do is get out of here right now and keep ahead of them."

"Then as soon as I saddle the mare, I'll be ready."

He gave her a hand. Then together they left the cave behind.

"We don't want to skyline ourselves," he said. "So instead of going over the mesa, we'll go around it. We'll put it between ourselves and Hatten, at least for a time."

"They're sure to trail us," she said. "What will we do?"

"Worry about it when the time comes."

The trail was narrow as Shad led the way. The side of the mesa was fairly steep and covered with mesquite, yucca, and chimaza. It offered some cover, but not nearly as much as he would have liked.

"How did you find me?" she asked.

He told her about their rescue attempts. "We had a couple of near misses," he said. "Then this last time we found that Hatten and the rest of his outfit had pulled out."

"He ordered an outlaw named Hodge to take me to that mesa hideout, kill me, and dispose of my body," she said. "Hodge wouldn't do it. He sent me on my way with a gun and supplies. Told me to ride for Trinidad. He went north toward Wyoming."

"We owe him," said Shad.

"I know. He put his own life in danger to release me. I hope they never find him."

The fog was finally a thing of the past. Shad looked over the plains and spotted four riders headed for the mesa. Even from a distance he could see that one of them was a woman.

"Here they come," he said. "Let's keep behind this scrub as much as possible. Maybe they won't see us from down there."

"I'm surprised there's only four," said Anne. "I would have thought they'd be out in full force."

"The rest went after Hodge."

"Oh, no," she said. "But I guess he was expecting it."

Shad thought the man a cut or two above Hatten and wished him well, but when you played with rattlesnakes, you ofttimes got bit.

They went on a little farther before Shad stopped and pulled a pair of field glasses from his pack. Taking care that the lenses didn't reflect sunlight to the outlaws, he took a good look. He was able to make out Gert. To her left was Avery Hatten. Next was a man he didn't recognize. Finally there was Hatten himself.

"It doesn't look good, does it?" she said as he returned the glasses to his pack.

"Not any worse than before."

"I'm wondering why you came after me all by yourself."

"I didn't. I simply got restless and came on ahead of the others. There's seven more who'll be starting out at dawn."

"I'm so grateful you got an early start."

"Come on," he said. "We'll work our way over to the

west end of the mesa. We can't afford to lose any more time."

"Lead on."

The going was rough, but the horses managed to pick their way along the rocky edge. Although it would have been much faster to descend and ride on the flatland, such a move would leave them exposed. They'd gone about a quarter of a mile when they had to divert from their path because a large boulder blocked the way. This chewed up time that they didn't have to spare, yet the boulder would serve as a barrier to sight as well as bullets. Once they were around it, he felt a little better. Not much, but a little.

Every so often he'd pause to listen. So far he couldn't hear them, but he was certain they were still following. Hatten wasn't about to let a fortune get away from him. At last they reached the end of the mesa and were able to turn south.

"This is the short side," he said. "We'll soon reach the south side and head back toward the east. Somewhere along the south slope we're going to have to find a place where we can make a stand. We're going to have to hold them off until my men can catch up."

The girl's tracks had washed out, but there was a fresh set that led up to a cave.

"Up there on the mesa," said Bray. "Looks like a good place for the girl to hide out. Maybe she's still there, and it might be she's not alone.

"Then let's go get 'em," said Hatten.

Bray led off, with Avery slightly behind him. Hatten came last behind Gert in order to keep an eye on her. When they finally reached the cave, it was empty.

Bray pointed to fresh horse droppings and the tracks around the opening. "For sure, there's two of 'em," he said.

"How can that be?" said Hatten.

"You tell me."

There was no denying it. The girl had an ally.

Bray went inside and sifted the ashes from the campfire through his fingers.

"Still warm," he announced. "Maybe one of Featherstone's men passed us by last night or this morning in the fog."

Hatten recalled that something had awakened him during the night. A noise maybe. Could have been the man who'd joined the Madison girl. Good thing the fire had gone out and they were down in a draw. Otherwise they'd have been sitting ducks.

"Those two can't have gone far," he said. "And they've left a trail that a blind man could follow."

No one was paying any attention to Avery when he aimed his rifle at the sky and squeezed off a shot. Hatten flinched at the noise. Then he walked over and grabbed the weapon from his nephew's hand.

"What do you think you're doing?" he demanded to know.

Avery took a step back, surprised by Hatten's reaction. "Why, I was just worrying them a little. Letting them know we're coming for them."

"Are you sure this dumb donkey ain't on their side?" said Bray.

Hatten gave his nephew a scathing look. "You just now went and warned 'em that we're here. Thanks to you our job is going to be that much harder."

Avery glanced from Bray to Hatten. No question about it, shooting that rifle off had been the wrong thing to do.

"We're wasting time," said Bray. "Do we want to catch up to 'em, or do we want to stand here passing the time of day?"

"Let's get going," said Hatten.

Shad and the Judge's daughter were on the west side of the mesa when they heard a rifle shot.

"Sounds like they've found the cave," he said. "That's not a healthy place to be, I'd wager."

Anne shuddered. "And to think, if you hadn't come along, I'd still be there."

He was glad he'd had that hunch to come on ahead. No doubt about it, a man's hunches often paid off.

Chapter Eleven

Having been relieved from guard duty by McNary, Abe lay sprawled on one of the bunks that lined the back wall of the hideout. He was deeply troubled, and, try as he might, he couldn't sleep. The hours slipped by. He scolded himself. *You never should have let Shad ride off like that on his own. You should have gone with him. Between the two of us, we might have stood a chance.*

Various rhythms of snoring filled the room. With the exception of McNary, all the men were dead to the world. He reckoned it was almost dawn. He took a deep breath and tried to quiet his mind. It didn't work. The air inside was stale, and he felt as if the walls were closing in on him. *I've got to get out of here,* he thought. He swung his legs over the side of the bunk and pulled on his boots. Then, after strapping on his pistol and grab-

158

bing his coat, he headed for the door. Outside he breathed deeply, savoring the fresh air. Low to the ground was a blanket of fog.

"That you, Abe?" said McNary, who was stationed several yards away.

"Yeah, it's me. I couldn't sleep."

McNary approached. "I know what you mean. It's a little crowded inside."

"I guess the real reason I couldn't sleep was because I'm worried about Shad and that girl. I shouldn't have let him take off on his own like that."

"Appears to me that Wakefield does pretty much what he pleases. I doubt if you could have stopped him."

What McNary said was true.

"There's something else you might ought to think about, Abe," he said. "I've noticed that Wakefield usually comes out on top. He's got his wits about him, and there's starch in his backbone. He's a man to have by your side when you're in trouble."

McNary was right, he conceded. Still, backbone and wits weren't always enough. You had to have some luck too.

"I've got a bad feeling about this, McNary. I don't think we should wait any longer to pull out of here."

"Whatever you say. But if you go in there and wake those fellows now, they're going to be as ornery as bears with thorns in their paws."

"Maybe so. Still, I don't aim to sit around here twiddling my thumbs when Shad and that girl are in trouble."

Suddenly McNary clamped a hand on his shoulder. "Listen!"

Abe strained to hear through the sound-muffling fog. There were riders coming from the north. Hatten's men were returning.

"Blast it! That's all we need right now."

"I'll alert the men," said McNary.

It didn't take them long to pull on their boots and arm themselves. Abe started issuing orders. "Dobbs, you come with McNary and me. We'll climb up onto the mesa above the hideout. If we divide up, we'll stand a better chance. Montoya, you secure the horses. Try to keep them calm. Lemke, go with him and help. Rutledge, you and Crane stay put inside. Don't start firing until we do. They don't know we're here."

"Will do, boss," said Rutledge, acknowledging that Abe was in command in Shad's absence.

Abe led McNary and Dobbs up the steep slope until they were above the hideout. Daylight was trying to edge out the fog. In the half light they hunkered down behind a tumble of rocks and a thicket of knee-high snowberry bushes. From that vantage point Abe could make out half a dozen fog-shrouded figures riding toward the shack.

"Hold your fire," he whispered. "Let them get closer."

He steadied the Henry repeater and watched until the riders were well within range. Then he squeezed off a shot that landed just short of the lead rider. The startled horse nearly threw him, and the morning air was filled with curses.

"Hatten!" yelled one of them. "Cut it out! It's us!"

It was McNary's rifle that answered. A barrage of gunfire followed. Seeing through the wispy trails of fog wasn't easy, but Abe aimed at the flashes of light. The men in the hideout had joined the battle. So had Lemke and Montoya.

Suddenly the shooting tapered off. It was now fully light, and Abe could see that the enemy was dividing. Half were staying put, but the others were circling around, using the low-lying fog for cover. If they got higher on the mesa, it would mean big trouble.

McNary spotted them too. "They're going to try to get above us," he said.

"We'll have to stop them, then," said Abe. "You take that first one. I'll take the second."

Their shots sounded almost as one. The nearest outlaw lurched backward and fell out of the saddle. The other one slumped as if wounded, but he managed to hang on and make it back to the others. The third man, however, disappeared from sight.

Abe toted it up. One dead. One badly wounded. One unaccounted for. Three others were out there on the plains.

"Looks like they're backing off," said McNary. "The fog's clearing, and it's broad daylight. They've got no cover now."

"I'm worried about the one who got to the mesa."

"Then what do you say we go and make him welcome?"

The three of them split up and worked their way

northward. They kept low, using any available cover. Dobbs was highest on the mesa. Below him, moving along a parallel path, came McNary. Abe was lowest. He kept watch for any movement that would give the outlaw away and was first to spot him. The man was hunkered down behind some sagebrush.

"You, there!" Abe called. "Give it up! Your friends have gone off and abandoned you. Now, you don't want to die up here all by your lonesome, do you?"

"Go to blazes!" came the reply.

Abe saw the barrel of his gun come up, and he slid downhill to get out of the way just as the outlaw fired. The bullet missed him by inches. McNary, who hadn't been spotted, was close. He stood. His .44 was aimed at the outlaw's head.

"Lay down your gun, easy-like now," he ordered.

Because he had no choice, the man did as he was told. McNary and Dobbs moved in quickly. While they bound the captive's hands, Abe went back to where the outlaw's horse had been tied and gathered the reins.

"Let's get down to the others," he said.

With horse and prisoner in tow, they headed for the lean-to stable beside the shack. There they found Montoya and Crane kneeling over the prone body of Lemke. There was blood all over the front of Lemke's shirt.

"His wound is a bad one," said Montoya.

"Better carry him inside," said Abe. "We've got to get that bleeding stopped."

"Am I done for?" asked Lemke, his voice weak.

"Nah," said Abe. "We've just got to plug up a hole or two, that's all. You'll be fit as a new Sunday suit before you know it."

Gently they carried the wounded man inside and placed him on a pallet.

Montoya took Abe aside. "I do not like the looks of it, *Señor* Featherstone. I've seen wounds like this one before."

Abe knew that Montoya had a good deal of experience doctoring such things. More than any of the others.

"I'd be obliged if you'd do what you can for him," he said.

Montoya nodded. "Of course, *señor,* I will try. But it is in God's hands now."

Lemke's breathing was labored, and he was in considerable pain. Montoya began to work on him. McNary built up a fire in the fireplace and put a pot of water on to boil. It was then they heard gunshots in the distance.

"What now?" said Crane. "Sounds like war has broken out again."

Abe opened the door a crack and looked outside.

"See anything?" asked McNary.

"Something's going on. There's a bunch of 'em out there shooting at one another. I'm going to have me a closer look. Dobbs, keep an eye on the prisoner."

Abe picked up his rifle and slipped outside. McNary followed.

"I'm thinking that must be Baca and his men," said Abe. "The sheriff must have decided to deal himself in. Looks like he's run smack-dab into Hatten's outfit."

They didn't have to wait long to find out what had happened. First the gunfire stopped. Then the posse came riding up to the hideout. Baca was in the lead. He'd taken prisoners.

"Good morning," said Abe. "I see you've had good hunting."

"You might say that. What about yourself?"

"That bunch rode up here a little while ago, just before dawn. I guess they were going to meet Hatten here. We had a shoot-out. Captured one of 'em. Got him inside, trussed up good and proper. There's another one lying out there dead somewhere. One of ours got wounded. It's Lemke. Montoya is in there doctoring him right now."

"Too bad," said Baca. "We were lucky. All my men survived. But what of the Judge's daughter? Did you find her?"

"No, but one of Hatten's outlaws brought her to this place. We think he had orders to kill her and hide the body. But they split up once they got here. He went north, and she headed south. Anyway, that's the way the signs read. Trouble was, the outlaws followed. Guess they decided to make sure the first fellow did the job right. Some of 'em rode north. Four of 'em went south after the girl. Shad left last night to try to find her. We were going to pull out at first light."

"Then these sorry fellows must be the ones who came back from the north," said Baca.

The prisoners were tied and thrown over the backs of their horses like sacks of potatoes. Abe noticed that one of them wasn't bound like the others. A second look told him there was no need. He was dead.

"That one's name is Chester Smith," said Baca, who'd noticed his interest. "At least that's what one of 'em told me. He said that Smith had recently come down from Denver."

"He must be the owl-hoot who kidnapped Anne," said Abe. "I figure he got what's coming to him."

"They all will, if I have anything to say about it," said Baca.

"Well, you've sure got my vote next time you need it."

"Gracias, amigo."

"What about that Ute woman who was cooking for Hatten and his bunch?" said Abe.

"We saw no sign of her, but someone said she took off on her own. Probably went back to her own people."

Abe was eager to get started. "You coming with us, Baca?" he asked.

"Alas, no. I'm needed in Trinidad, and I must get these prisoners behind bars. I'll take a more direct route, but I'll leave a couple of my men behind to help Montoya. Sanchez is very good with bullet wounds."

"Again, I'm in your debt," said Abe.

"Before you go," said Baca, "I'd best deputize you and your men. That way your actions will be legal. As of now, you're working for me."

"Never aspired to be a lawman," said Abe. "My best friend wore a badge and got a bullet for his trouble." Shadrach's father.

"That is one of the hazards of the job, *amigo.*"

Baca commandeered a badge from one of his deputies and tossed it to Abe. "This will have to do, I'm afraid. You can vouch for the others, or they can let their guns do the vouching for them."

Abe put the badge into the pocket of his vest and called his men. "Saddle up! All except for Montoya. He's staying with Lemke."

When Abe rode south that morning, McNary, Dobbs, Rutledge, and Crane rode alongside him.

Meanwhile, Hatten and the other three followed the trail of Anne Madison and the man who was with her. Jed squinted into the distance, trying to catch sight of his quarry, but the mesa was rugged and overgrown with scrub. It offered no clear view. They rode single file with Bray, the best tracker, in the lead. Hatten followed. Next came Gert. Avery was last so he could keep an eye on her.

They hadn't gone far when a boulder blocked their path. Bray cat-hopped his mount to higher ground so he could go around the obstruction.

"Come on!" the gunman called. "They went this way."

Hatten and the others followed Bray's lead. It appeared that the girl and her partner were keeping to the high ground rather than making a run for it across the plains. That was going to make their capture more difficult. Whoever the fellow was, he was savvy.

Hatten's mood was grim. It was his bad luck that the girl wasn't alone. Otherwise she'd have been easy pickings. Still, he wasn't about to let her get away. Anne Madison was his last chance to salvage something before he headed west. Capturing her would mean enough money for a new start.

"Can't you hurry it up, Bray?" he prodded.

The gunman ignored him, continuing at the same pace. Hatten fumed. If it had been anybody else . . .

The sky was clear now. All signs of yesterday's storm and the morning's fog were gone. Any water that hadn't been absorbed by the arid land had long since evaporated. A brisk wind blew down from the north, battering the exposed slope of the mesa. Hatten hunched his shoulders, wishing he was on the sheltered side.

He thought of his men and wondered if they'd succeeded in killing the traitor Hodge. The man's death was important, so important that he'd put a price on his head. If it had been foolish for him to divide his forces, then so be it. Nobody betrayed Jed Hatten and lived to brag about it.

"I still don't see any sign of 'em," said Bray. "They must have gotten a bigger start than we thought."

"Then you'd better quit jawin' and keep going," said Hatten.

He glanced over his shoulder and saw that Gert and Avery were following close behind him.

She noticed his look. "I don't understand why the two of 'em didn't get off this mesa and ride on the flats, where it's easier going," she complained.

Hatten didn't answer. To him the reason was obvious.

He felt a growing sense of unease. With a lead like they had, his quarry could lie in wait and dry-gulch their pursuers. He wouldn't have worried about the girl on her own, but now she had a partner, one who knew his way around. Had Hatten been in their place, dry-gulching was exactly what he would do.

Anne was feeling more hopeful than she had since the day of her kidnapping. For the first time she wasn't alone. Shad Wakefield was with her. And if everything her father had said about him was true, he was an exceptionally strong ally. Still, she was troubled.

"They can't be far behind us," she said.

"I reckon not."

"Then wouldn't it be better for us to get down off this mountainside and head straight for Trinidad?"

He glanced back at her. "It'd be dangerous. We'd be making ourselves easy targets if we tried. We'd end up running the horses to death out on the open ground, where we'd have no cover. When our ammunition gave out, all Hatten and his partners would have to do is ride up and shoot us, or take you captive again."

The picture he'd evoked was a chilling one.

"What are we going to do, then?" she asked.

"The way I see it, the best chance we've got is to put this mesa between ourselves and the outlaws. They'll follow, of course. But in the meantime we'll have a chance to look for cover. Find a place we can defend. Then we'll have to hold them off until Abe can get here with the others."

He pulled out his pocket watch and checked the time. If they'd left at daybreak, the men would be hours behind, though they'd be able to make better time in the daylight than he had in the dark.

He sorely needed sleep. Still, he thanked whatever had prodded him to leave the night before. Had he not come on ahead, Anne would now be recaptured—or dead.

"Do you have any idea where we are?" she asked.

"I'm sorry to say that we're still a long ride from Trinidad. If I'm not mistaken, we're not far from the Apishapa River."

"I guess no one will be coming from Trinidad to help us, then."

"It isn't likely. Should Sheriff Baca decide to raise a posse, he'd lead it up to Hatten's place."

Shad considered the situation from the outlaw's point of view. Hatten would know there were two of them now. He'd also realize that word was out about the murder and kidnapping. When it spread, he'd be hunted. After what he'd done, he would find no refuge. He'd have to leave Colorado altogether to keep his neck from being stretched. His best bet for getting his hands on some money was to capture Anne and hold her for ransom. No doubt he was feeling desperate, and desperate men were often the most dangerous of all.

Chapter Twelve

Abe and the others rode hard to make up for lost time. The fog had burned off, and Shad's trail was easy to follow. McNary left them from time to time, outriding in search of any sign of the outlaws. They'd put some distance between themselves and the hideout when they heard McNary shout.

"Over here! I think I've found where Hatten and three others were camped."

When they got there, it was plain to see that a fire had been built in the draw. Abe also noticed where they'd staked their horses. There were footprints too. Lots of them. One set belonged to a woman.

"There were four of 'em, all right," said Crane. "Wakefield must have passed by awful close without knowing they were here. I expect they'd let the fire die out, and they were all asleep at the time."

"I do believe that boy was born under a lucky star," said Abe.

"He might not think he's so lucky when they catch up with him," said Crane.

Abe noticed the assumption Shad's former enemy was making, and he didn't like it one little bit. "Then we'd better not let that happen," he said. "Let's get a move on."

They followed the outlaws' trail until it merged with Shad's. Abe figured Hatten could read that sign as well as he had. He'd know that somebody had gotten ahead of him and was between him and Anne Madison.

When Abe saw a scrub-covered mesa looming in the distance, it started him to thinking. "Anne would have been caught in that rainstorm," he said. "She'd have looked for shelter, and there's nothing around but that mesa up ahead."

"Makes sense to me that she'd try to find an overhang or someplace dry to hole up," said McNary. "Let's go see."

If Anne had sheltered there, Abe hoped she hadn't lingered. Not with Hatten on her trail. It wasn't long before he spotted a cave and pointed it out. When they got to the base of the mesa, he reined in his horse.

"We'd better go up there and have a look," he said.

Single file, they made their way to the opening. At the cave entrance McNary climbed down and took a look inside. Abe leaned over his saddle horn and studied the tracks.

"Somebody stayed in there long enough to build a

fire," said McNary. "The ashes are cool now. A good sign, I think. And there were two of 'em."

"Well, they had some company," said Abe. "But maybe Hatten's men got here after Shad and the girl were safely away."

"Their trail leads west along this northern slope," said McNary. "We'd better get moving."

Abe tried to put himself in Shad's place and think like him. It appeared that his friend didn't have a lot of choices. He needed to stick to the mesa and work his way around to the slope that faced in the direction of Trinidad. The best thing he could do then would be to hole up and fend off the outlaws until reinforcements arrived. It was Abe's job to see that those reinforcements got there in time.

They soon came to a large boulder that obstructed the path. There were tracks where others had gone around it. Abe led his men in following those tracks.

"I hope you know what you're doing," said Crane.

The man never ceased to be irritating, thought Abe. "I'm following a trail," he said.

"If you've got an idea where they're going," said McNary, "I think it'd save some time if we went down and rode on the flat. The going would be easier."

Abe was reluctant to leave the trail. He wasn't sure the time they'd save was worth the risk of overlooking something. But in this case every minute could mean life or death.

"All right, let's do it," he said.

Once they were back on the flatland, they urged their mounts forward.

Shad and Anne found themselves on the south side of the mesa at last. Here they were sheltered from the north wind, which was no small comfort. He scanned the heights, looking for a place to hide, a position he could defend. They'd heard the shot that had been fired and knew how much of a lead they had.

They picked their way along the narrow, rocky trail, which had grown more difficult to follow. It soon began to lead them upward, and it wasn't long before Shad spotted what he'd been looking for.

"Up there," he said, pointing to an outcropping that had only a hint of a ledge around it. "That looks like a good place."

"Are you sure?" said Anne. "It doesn't look like much."

"Maybe not, but it might just save our bacon."

The climb was steep for McBeth and the mare. At one point the mare slid back a ways. But she was game. She dug in and kept on climbing. When they got to the outcrop, they faced a ledge that was barely wide enough for a horse to walk.

"Wait here," said Shad. "I'll take the sorrel around it first, and then I'll come back for you."

He dismounted and led McBeth around the obstacle. The drop-off was long and sheer. He dared not look down. Thankfully a dozen steps covered the distance.

When he reached the other side, he secured the horse to a mesquite bush before returning.

"I'll take the mare this time," he said, "and bring you over next. You're not afraid of heights, are you?"

She brushed a strand of hair from her face and looked up at him. "No. I'm afraid of falling from heights. But don't you worry about me. If you can walk across that narrow thing, so can I."

"Good," he said. "I'm counting on you."

He caught up the reins of the mare and started across. But it turned out she wasn't pleased about following him. He sweet-talked the nervous animal and, step by step, got her to the other side. When he started back for Anne, she was already halfway along. She was bellied up against the boulder so she couldn't look down and was inching her way toward him. He took a few steps and reached out for her.

"Grab my hand," he said.

When she took hold of it, he guided her on across.

"This is it?" she said.

"This is it. We'll have to make the best of it until help arrives. It's not exactly a fort, but the boulder will act as a shield unless they can get above or beyond it, and that won't be easy.

Hatten nearly fell out of his saddle when he heard the second shot. It was close, and it was at his back. He drew his gun without thinking.

"What in blazes . . ."

He turned and saw Gert's pale, frightened face.

Avery still held the pistol that he'd fired. The smell of sulphur tainted the air.

"What in thunder are you shooting at now?" Hatten demanded. "You scared me out of ten years."

"A rattlesnake. It was sunning itself up on that rock." Avery pointed to a spot that was now empty of life.

"Well, it ain't there now. Couldn't you have left it alone?"

"It was poisonous. It might have struck one of us."

Hatten felt a wave of disgust. "This is the second time you've warned them two up ahead. Thanks to you, they know right where we are."

Avery looked sullen.

"Stop and think before you pull another harebrained stunt like that," said Hatten. "You give us away again, and I might decide to shoot you and be done with it."

He noticed that Bray had half turned in his saddle in order to witness the exchange. His expression was cold and superior. Hatten wanted to wipe that smirk off his face—and would have, if he'd dared. The gunman made him feel as if he'd been caught in an act of stupidity himself.

"What is it you're staring at?" he challenged. "Turn around and get on with the job that I'm paying you to do."

Without a word Bray turned and rode on.

Hatten was now on the south side of the mesa. He looked over the plain below to make sure his quarry hadn't left the slope and made a run for it. There was no sign of them. *They're still up here somewhere. But where?*

* * *

Avery's gunshot warned Shad that the enemy was close.

"I can't see them yet," he said, "but stay back, and keep your pistol ready."

The big Colt revolver looked huge in Anne's small hand. But there was a look of determination on her face that told him she would use it willingly if she had to. She rested it against the boulder.

He'd taken both horses farther along and secured them at a wider part of the ledge. It was the best he could do. He readied the Henry repeater. There had been no time to cover their tracks, but from this height he had a clear view of the mesa below.

"So now we wait?" she said.

"Now we wait."

"I'm lucky to be here, so I shouldn't complain. When Hatten sent me away with Hodge, I knew he'd been ordered to kill me. I thought about escaping, but there simply wasn't any chance."

"Must have been rough," said Shad.

"Yes. I couldn't have been more surprised when Hodge let me go. He said he'd never killed a woman, and he didn't intend to start. He provided me with this gun, the mare, food, and water. Even a poncho to keep the rain off. Told me where to go while he rode north, probably to draw them away from me."

"It appears the man had a lot of good in him," said Shad.

"Yes, and I'll always be grateful."

"Hodge might be in for some trouble, though. Those

men Hatten sent north most likely have orders to find and kill him."

A look of alarm crossed her face. "I pray that saving my life won't condemn him to die. He's better than all the rest of them put together."

"You'll get no argument from me. But don't worry. If this Hodge is half the man I think he is, he won't be easy to kill."

He wished Hodge well. Still, his concern right now was his own survival, and that of Anne Madison.

Hatten knew this was his last chance. He couldn't afford to fail again. "You finding their tracks?" he asked Bray.

"Yep. I'm following them."

"Be careful," said Gert. "I don't want them shooting at me."

That had been worrying Hatten too. Anne Madison and her partner would be desperate and fighting for their lives. They wouldn't hold back.

Single file, they were making their way across the south slope when Bray suddenly stopped.

"What is it?" said Hatten. "What do you see?"

"They went up there," he said. "Likely they're holed up behind that outcrop. That's where I'd be anyway, if I was in that fellow's shoes."

Hatten shaded his eyes and looked up. He didn't like it. They'd be hard to dislodge from a place like that. But if worse came to worst, he could outwait them. Let them spend their bullets and run out of food and water.

Then they'd be easy pickings. Still, he couldn't afford to wait too long.

Suddenly he heard a gunshot. Dirt geysered in front of Bray's gelding. The startled horse reared, nearly unseating its rider. While Bray struggled to regain control, the others slid from their saddles and hit the dirt.

"They're behind that outcrop for sure," said Avery.

Hatten slipped his rifle from its boot. Then he got to one knee and took aim at the top of the stone barrier. He figured it was just within range, and when he glimpsed a piece of flannel, he squeezed off a shot. Bray followed suit.

Gunfire was spooking the horses. They were stamping and blowing, eyes wide with fear.

"Avery, take them animals back down the trail and tie 'em to something," Hatten ordered. "Then get back up here and help."

It was the first part of the order that Avery obeyed.

Bray crawled over and bellied up against the mesa wall. The angle made him a difficult target from above. Hatten was quick to do the same. He glanced at Gert and saw that she was hugging the ground.

The shooting had stopped, at least for a time. Whoever was up there was canny, and he wasn't inclined to waste ammunition on poor targets. A minute passed and then another. An eternity for a man like Hatten, who had little patience. He found himself sweating. He thought of Avery and wondered what was keeping him. He decided that the kid would never be worth what it took to feed him.

"Must have gone to sleep up there," said Bray.

"Well, maybe we ought to wake 'em up."

They both fired once, then twice. But all they managed to do was make a lot of noise, for their targets were well protected by the rock. Hatten wanted the girl alive anyway. It was her protector he had to get rid of.

"This ain't working," he told Bray. "We've got to get up above and shoot down on 'em, and we can't hit the girl."

"All right," said Bray. "You go first."

Hatten glared at him. "I'm paying you to follow my orders."

Bray stared back. "Look, you don't have enough money to pay for your own pine box," he said. "And without my help you're not apt to get any more."

Hatten felt his face grow red. He choked back a curse, for what the gunman said hit too close to home.

"All right," he said. "You stay here and cover me. I'm going up there."

He slung his rifle over his back and began crawling. Yard by yard he made his way up the side of the mesa. He used the scrub for cover and hoped that whoever was up there wouldn't notice him. He figured it was likely to be Wakefield and began picturing his unseen foe's face. He'd made it about forty yards when a bullet plowed into the ground in front of him. Dirt particles stung his eyes. He slid back, letting gravity carry him to the others.

He wiped the dirt from his eyes with the tail of his shirt. When he could see again, he spotted Avery duck-walking up to join them.

"Where have you been, boy?" he demanded. "You've been gone so long that I figured you'd turned yellow and run off."

Avery flushed at the insult. "You didn't tell me it was going to be like this," he said. "It was supposed to be easy. That girl would be alone, you said. Alone and unarmed. Now somebody's shooting at us. I could get killed."

"Yep," said Hatten. "And for my money that fellow up there is Shad Wakefield."

Avery got a sick look on his face. "Wakefield can shoot better'n most, and he don't back down. He cleaned out that land-grabbing outfit up north a few years back."

"Well, that's what we're up against."

"But there's only two of them and four of us," said Bray. "Three of us," he amended after a look at Gert, who was huddled against the side of the mesa.

"Yeah," said Hatten. "Maybe we can still pull this off."

Chapter Thirteen

S had missed his target, but having forced the outlaw down the slope, he felt that he'd won the first round. They'd try again, of course. It was only a question of when.

From his place behind the boulder he tried to spot them, but they were keeping out of sight. To his way of thinking, waiting was almost as bad as fighting. On the other hand, nothing was as bad as dodging bullets.

The young woman beside him was pale but composed even after being shot at. She was Harley Madison's daughter, and he trusted she'd be up to dealing with whatever happened. Her father would have been proud of her.

"None of those people has a conscience," said Anne so softly that he had to strain to hear her. "My life means nothing to them. Nor yours."

"I sure can't argue with you there."

He ran his hand over the dark, satiny wood of his rifle stock. After that first exchange of gunfire, a calmness had settled. Still, it was no comfort to him, for it was like the calm before a storm. He noticed a few puffy clouds drifting across an otherwise clear sky. The sun was warming the southern exposure of the mesa, and the north wind was effectively blocked. He checked the time. It would be a while before Abe and the others could arrive. Once they saw the outlaws' tracks, they'd know he was in trouble and would ride with all possible haste. He hoped they'd get here soon enough.

Overhead, a red-tailed hawk glided in a leisurely circle, checking them out. It was a beautiful creature, he thought, and it seemed so carefree. When its curiosity was satisfied, it flew on, leaving the humans to deal with their own problems in their own way.

The warning came when a mule deer leaped from cover below them and bounded away. Shad shifted his weight and steadied the rifle barrel on the outcrop.

"They're coming," he said.

No sooner were the words out than a bullet caromed off the rock face. Shad returned fire. He heard Anne firing too. The outlaws were still trying to make their way to a position above them. That way they could shoot down, and he and Anne would have no protection. No chance to survive. Shad had to keep them from gaining the high ground.

He worked the lever of the rifle. All thought was

gone, and there was nothing but desperate action. Then suddenly he felt a blow to his arm. Glancing down, he saw that his sleeve was wet with blood. He'd been hit.

"Keep firing," he told Anne. Then he pulled off his bandana and wrapped it around his arm above the wound. Anne stopped long enough to tie it for him, then resumed her post.

Shad knew that shock was keeping him from feeling any pain. A good thing. The outlaws had probably figured out that something was wrong, that possibly he was wounded or even dead. The lull in firing had been too long. No doubt they'd be moving in.

He threw up the rifle and levered three quick shots to let them know he was able. *Ought to slow 'em down a little,* he thought.

"We're not going to make it, are we?" said Anne after the brief barrage.

"Sure we will. Remember? We have reinforcements coming."

Still, those reinforcements were far off, and there was the matter of surviving until they arrived.

Again the shooting stopped. The way he had it figured, the outlaws were still trying to move upward. He had to find a way to protect Anne.

"Come with me," he said. He led her back a few yards to where a narrow overhang jutted out above the ledge.

"Stay under this," he said. "This will offer a little protection if they start shooting down on us from above.

"Well, it's fine for me," she said. "But what are you going to do?"

"I'm going to try to lead Hatten away."

She clutched his hand. "You can't do that, Shad. You've been hurt. If you leave here, they'll kill you."

Maybe she was right. But he simply had no choice.

"I'll be fine," he assured her. "Just stay put, and don't worry. Keep that gun ready too."

He slung the rifle over his shoulder. His revolver was in its holster, and the knife was in his belt. Anne clutched Hodge's .44 and looked determined to use it.

"If any of 'em get close, shoot 'em," he said. "Don't think about it. Just squeeze the trigger.

"I will," she promised. "I know it's them or us."

Leaving her, he moved on. The shock that had set in when he was first hit was wearing off, and his arm hurt like all get out. But at least the bleeding had stopped. For a time, anyway.

Gingerly he made his way past the horses, then eastward along the mesa wall. When he figured that he'd gone far enough, he stopped. For a time the outcrop would shield him from sight. Now he would climb.

The mesa was steep here, exposing rock that had only sparse vegetation. He found a foothold, a mere chink in the mesa wall. Grabbing a handful of scrubby mesquite, he hoisted himself up, favoring his wounded arm.

Above his head was a larger crack in the wall. He reached up with his good arm and grabbed hold. Another toehold bore part of his weight as he pulled himself upward. He'd almost made it when his foot slipped. For an instant he hung in midair, suspended above the flatland far below. He dared not look down. Desperately he reached down with his other hand and grabbed the knife from his belt. With a quick motion he plunged it into the side of the mesa, creating another handhold. This took enough pressure off his arm that he was able to steady himself and find a narrow footing.

Both arms ached, and his breathing was heavy from the exertion. His heart pounded after his close call with death. He paused for a moment. From this position he was clearly visible to the outlaws below. One of them— it looked like Hatten—aimed his rifle and fired. The bullet fell short. Shooting uphill with accuracy was hard to do, and he was almost out of range. But clinging to the slope as he was rendered him helpless to fight back. He needed to reach the ledge above. Handhold by handhold he climbed, ignoring the guns below, until at last he heaved his body onto the ledge.

He took a moment to catch his breath. His shirt was wet, and he saw that his wound had started seeping blood again. He tore off a piece of his sleeve and stuffed it under the bandana. Otherwise there was no help for it.

From where he sat, he could see very little of Anne. The overhang covered most of her from this angle. It would hide all of her from anyone farther west. Then he spotted Hatten on the move. He was heading straight for the boulder. Soon the same rock that had shielded Shad would shield his enemy.

"Give it up, girl!" the outlaw called. "Tell your

friend, Wakefield, to throw away his gun and come down here. We'll let him go."

She met his offer with silence.

Shad couldn't see or get a shot at the outlaw now, which was what the fellow had planned.

"Looks like Wakefield ain't comin' down," said Hatten. "Why don't you be smart, girl, and come on out? We ain't going to hurt you. We're just going to get a little money for you, that's all. And you've got plenty to spare."

Still silence.

"Look," said Hatten, growing impatient, "I'm not going to kill you, if that's what you're afraid of. I'm just going to ask for a few dollars' ransom."

While Shad listened, something started niggling at him. The others had been quiet for too long. They had to be up to something.

His attention had been on the outcrop that hid Hatten from his rifle fire. Now he glanced directly downward. The outlaw's gunman was below Anne and climbing straight toward her. Hatten's talk about surrender had merely been a diversion.

They all knew where he was. Still, he'd crawled a ways, and he'd be hard to spot. His shirt and pants blended with the colors of the mesa.

He drew a bead on the climbing gunman. But before he could fire, he was overcome by a wave of dizziness. He took a breath and tried to clear his head. Sweat had popped out on his forehead, and blood soaked his makeshift bandage. Overhead, a buzzard circled low, searching for a meal. He silently willed it to leave. Almost as if it had heard Shad's thoughts, the large bird made one more circle before heading out in the direction of the river.

Shad looked down to find that Hatten had moved to a position above the rock outcrop and was closing in on Anne. She was caught between him and the gunman. Hatten was making himself a difficult target by lying flat and using scrub for cover.

The other outlaw was now directly below Anne, and he posed the greatest danger. Shad had a clear shot. Again he aimed the rifle. This time he fired. The gunman looked up. He was hit, but he managed to hold on, two seconds, three, four. Then he fell into space. His scream echoed against the mesa.

Hatten fired up at Shad, but his camouflage was effective. The bullet hit his leg but was partially deflected by his boot.

Shad returned fire, but Hatten had slid down far enough to put the edge of the outcrop between them.

"Hatten, if you're looking for me, come on out!" he called. "I'm right here."

The outlaw kept to his hiding place.

"Wakefield!" he called. "You've been a troublemaker from the first. Now you're going to die."

Shad waited. Nothing happened. He wondered where the nephew and the woman had gotten off to. How were they going to play out this hand? For his own part, he was weak from blood loss and fearful that he would lose consciousness.

Minutes passed. Then Shad saw the barrel of Hatten's rifle emerge at the edge of the outcrop. He was prepared when the outlaw quickly stepped out to fire a shot. He levered one of his own. Hatten's shot missed. His didn't. Hatten fell backward, sliding a short distance down the slope of the mesa. Even from a distance Shad could see a dark stain spreading over the front of Hatten's shirt.

That was the last thing he remembered before everything started going black. His final thought was of Anne. *Can she protect herself from the other two? She was simply going to have to.*

Chapter Fourteen

It was colder than a banker's heart, and Shad was shivering so hard that his teeth were chattering. He wanted a blanket, a coat, anything to warm him. The inside of his mouth was dry as flannel. He needed a drink in the worst way. His eyelids were heavy, and it was too much of an effort to open them. How much time had passed, he didn't know. Neither could he recall where he was. As he lay there, familiar voices began to drift across his consciousness. One of them belonged to Dan McNary.

"Looks like he's been shot twice," said his foreman. "The wound in his arm has bled a lot. The other is a graze just above his boot."

Shad struggled again to open his eyes.

"It's going to be ticklish getting him down off this

ledge," McNary went on. "He's going to be dead weight too, but at least he's alive."

Shad's memory clicked in, and he began to recall what had happened before he blacked out.

Hatten and his gunman are dead. But what about the others? What about Avery and that woman? Have they taken Anne away?

"Anne?" he managed to say. "Where is she?"

"It's about time you was comin' around," said Abe, who'd joined McNary. "Sorry we got here too late to take part in the festivities."

Shad opened his eyes and tried to sit up. "Glad to see you, late or not. Is Anne all right?"

"Right as rain," said Abe. "We sent her on down with Crane and the horses. Didn't want her up here making a big fuss over you."

"Now we've got to get you down from here," said McNary.

It turned out to be a lot easier than any of them expected. Shad's main fear was that he'd black out again. McNary went first to block them if they slid. Next came Shad and Abe together. Abe steadied him while Shad favored his injured leg. Little by little they eased their way downward.

The others were waiting when they got there.

Anne rushed up to him. "You look awful," she said. "These men arrived before I could get to you, and they pretty much took over."

"I'm fine," he tried to assure her, knowing full well how bad he must look.

He saw that Gertie Bacon and Avery Hatten were prisoners. Their hands were bound, and Rutledge was guarding them. The Bacon woman wore a sullen expression, and Avery was the picture of despair.

"Look, your wounds need attention right away," said Anne.

"A drink first," said Shad, "and a blanket."

"Maybe some whiskey," said Abe, as Anne hurried to get what was asked. "I'll take care of the doctoring part."

He cleaned the arm wound and poured alcohol onto it. The alcohol caused Shad to wince. Then Abe added fresh padding and a bandage.

"That should take care of any more blood loss," he said.

The leg wound was superficial and required little attention.

Shad wrapped the blanket around his shoulders and gulped the drink that was offered.

"That gunman you killed was named Bray," said McNary. "He was a bad one. I guess you know you killed Hatten too."

Then the Judge's murderer was dead. Justice was done. Shad could live with that.

"What about the outlaws who rode north?" he asked.

"They came back before we could get onto your trail. We got them too. At least we started it. Baca and his posse ended it."

"Baca?"

"Yep. Him and his men went to Hatten's place to rescue Anne. They found 'em gone and followed their trail to the hideout. On the way they ran into the outlaws after we'd already had one go-around with them."

"I wonder what happened to Hodge, the fellow who let Anne go," said Shad.

"According to one of Baca's prisoners, they didn't find him. He got clean away."

"I'm glad," said Anne, who was listening. "I owe him my life."

Shad figured that maybe Hodge had gotten justice too.

"If you're up to riding," said Abe, "I expect we'd better start heading home."

Shad was sore, wounded, and bone weary, but he wanted away from this place. If he could sit a saddle, he intended to ride.

He noticed that Lemke and Montoya were missing and asked about them.

"Lemke's badly wounded," said Abe. "He's got a chance though, and Montoya's with him. Baca left a fellow who's good at doctoring too. So with both of 'em looking after him, he's got the best care possible."

Shad felt bad for Lemke. He'd known him for years. He also knew that Montoya was good at taking care of broken bones and gunshot wounds and was glad that he was at Lemke's side.

It was almost dusk when they left the mesa. They stopped and made camp a few miles beyond. Abe brewed up some hot tea and gave it to Shad, saying that tea was good for shock and blood loss. He drank it and managed to get down some bacon and pan bread too.

When they bedded down for the night, guard duty

was assigned to the able-bodied. That left Shad out. He was too tired to argue. He crawled beneath his blankets, closed his eyes, and went to sleep.

It was still dark when he was awakened by a noise. For a moment he lay there listening, trying to figure out what it was and where it had come from. Several yards away the flames of the campfire had burned down to embers. Only the moon and a sprinkling of stars were left to light the prairie.

Slowly he turned his head to the right and glimpsed a shadow moving toward the horses. Strangely, no one appeared to be on watch. Shad grasped the revolver at his side. Then, as quickly and quietly as he could, he rolled out of his blankets and got up. From there he crept in stocking feet across the clearing. But before he could reach his destination, he tripped. Falling to his knees, he discovered an unconscious Rutledge stretched out on the ground. Avery Hatten was escaping. He shouted the alarm.

He heard the men scrambling out of their blankets as he got back to his feet. He ran toward the horses. Avery was saddling McBeth.

"Hold it!" Shad ordered. "I've got you covered."

Avery dropped into a squat and fired off two quick shots in his direction. But Shad was already running a zigzag course toward the remuda.

"Give it up, Avery!" he shouted.

The outlaw swung into the saddle and took off to the north. Unwilling to shoot at Avery in the moonlight and maybe hit McBeth by mistake, Shad held his fire.

McNary reached his mount, with Abe close behind. They quickly saddled the horses. But every minute gave Avery Hatten a bigger lead.

Shad went back to his bedroll and pulled on his boots.

Gert was still with them, and she was sitting there, wide awake. "He got away from you, didn't he?" she taunted.

"He's not in the clear yet," said Shad. "And what's it got to do with you, anyway? He left you behind."

"Avery's going to come back for me," she said. "You wait and see. He's always been sweet on me."

"If you say so," he replied.

Shad felt right next door to useless. All he could do was sit there and wait. Abe and McNary were doing all the work. Dobbs, Crane, Anne and he had nothing to do but guard the woman and see to Rutledge.

Crane built up the fire while Shad examined the injured man. He had a knot on the side of his head the size of a hickory nut.

"Rutledge," he said. "Wake up."

The only answer was a moan.

"I think he'll be coming around soon," said Dobbs. "The man has a hard head."

Anne came and sat beside Shad as he bathed Rutledge's face with water from a canteen. The rest was up to Nature. He hoped Dobbs was right and Rutledge did, indeed, have a hard head. One that could withstand a pistol-whipping with no permanent damage.

Crane put on a pot of coffee to boil. "If the smell of this don't wake him up," he said, "nothing will."

They were waiting for the coffee when, from the corner of his eye, Shad caught a slight movement beyond the outer edge of the firelight.

"Hold it, Gert!" he ordered, drawing his gun.

She ignored him, knowing he wouldn't shoot a woman, and ran. He swore and holstered the pistol. Not waiting for the others, he went after her. Each step on his wounded leg was a misery, but he'd be hanged if he'd let her get away. It took awhile, but he finally caught up with her and dragged her back. All the while she was spitting and clawing like a cat.

The others were waiting when he brought her into the firelight. Anne looked at her with pity, remembering the woman's one act of kindness in giving her the shawl.

"You've messed up everything for us, Wakefield," Gert accused. "If you'd done what you were supposed to and killed Kershaw right off, I'd soon be a rich, respected woman."

"I'm afraid, Gert, that you wouldn't have had much time to enjoy it," said Shad. "Hatten wasn't about to let you live once he got his hands on that ranch and the Judge's money. What's more, I think you're smart enough to have figured that out for yourself."

That shut her up. She looked downright dejected as she huddled near the fire, her hands still bound.

"Keep an eye on her," he told Dobbs. "We've got enough trouble without her sneaking off again."

He went to check on Rutledge. The man was moaning and muttering.

"Hey, it's me, Shad," he said. "Can you hear me?"

Rutledge mumbled a few unintelligible words. Then he opened his eyes and struggled to sit up.

"Take it easy, *amigo*," Shad cautioned. "You've had a bad blow to the head."

"What happened?" Rutledge asked.

"Avery Hatten got loose and knocked you out."

Rutledge reached up and touched the knot on his head, then winced in pain. "Did that no-good coyote get away?" he asked.

"For the time being. But Abe and McNary went after him. You just lie still and take it easy for awhile."

"That woman get away too?"

"No. She's right over there."

It was clear by her slumped shoulders and drooping head that Gert Bacon was a defeated, unhappy remnant of her former self. He doubted if she really expected Avery to come back for her. Avery had troubles enough of his own. Shad only hoped that during his getaway he didn't injure McBeth.

It was well past dawn when three riders approached camp. The one on McBeth was all trussed up. It appeared that Avery Hatten hadn't gotten very far.

When Gert spotted them riding in, she looked as if it were the end of the world. Her last hope, no matter how slim, was gone.

"How did you catch him?" asked Shad when the riders had dismounted.

"We ran him to ground back at the mesa," said Abe. "You'd think he'd have gotten his fill of it by now."

"How's Rutledge?" asked McNary.

"I'll live," said the injured man from his pallet, "but I've got one whale of a headache. I'd like to get my hands on that galoot. You'd better guard him close."

"Don't worry," said Abe. "Sheriff Baca is waiting for him. If Avery don't outright hang, he'll be in prison for a long time to come."

"Well, if everybody's able to ride," said Shad, "we'd better get a move on. It's still a long way to Trinidad."

They were all on short rations of sleep, and they took it slowly because of Shad's and Rutledge's injuries. It turned out that they had to make camp again on the open plains. This time they put a double guard on the prisoners and made sure that both their hands and their feet were bound.

It wasn't until late the morning after that they rode into Trinidad with Anne and the prisoners.

Their entourage aroused the curiosity of the towns-people, many of whom came out to watch as they rode by. When they saw the real Anne Madison, none of them could doubt her authenticity. In spite of her ordeal she'd managed to smooth her hair and put her clothes in order. What's more, she rode with her head up and back erect like the finest of ladies, which, of course, she was.

They reined up in front of the jail and tied their horses to the hitch rail. Sheriff Baca and his deputies had gotten back before them.

"Have you got a couple of empty cells, Baca?" asked Abe as he entered the sheriff's office.

"I've had them reserved," said Baca. "It's about time they were filled."

After the two prisoners were jailed, Anne was introduced to the sheriff. Then Abe and Shad told their stories.

"So Hatten and his gunman, Bray, are dead," said Baca. "I doubt very much if they'll be mourned. Certainly not by anyone around here."

"Before I forget," said Abe, "I've got something of yours." He pulled the badge from his pocket and tossed it onto the sheriff's desk.

"You did it honor," said Baca. "If I ever need a deputy, I'll know where to come."

Abe chuckled. "Now, don't get the wrong idea. I don't intend to make lawman's work a habit."

Baca nodded. "I understand," he said. "I've learned that it has its drawbacks."

He turned to Shad. "Perhaps you'd better see the doctor, Señor Wakefield."

"He's going there next," Abe assured him. "And we're obliged for your help."

Outside the jail, Luke Crane mounted up. "I'll be heading back to my ranch," he said. "Again, I appreciate the rescue."

Shad gave him the slightest of nods. He wasn't sorry to see Crane go. There was too much bad blood between them. Besides, it was hard to overlook the fact that Crane was the one who'd hired away the Judge's hands, making his murder possible. That act itself had been malicious, even if he hadn't realized how it would turn out. In his opinion those disloyal cowhands and Luke Crane deserved one another.

Now that the prisoners had been deposited with Baca, Shad sent Rutledge and Dobbs on ahead to the Lazy M with orders to prepare for the new owner. Next he stopped in at the doctor's office to get his wounds looked at, even though he figured Abe had done as good a job as any sawbones could.

"You were lucky," said Doc Gardner, a rotund man in his middle years, after he'd replaced the old bandages. "That bullet didn't do near as much damage to your arm as it could have. Worst part is you've lost a good deal of blood. It'll take some time to build it up. Your leg's not too bad at all. My advice to you is that next time you get shot at, be sure to duck."

Shad couldn't suppress a grin. He'd given that same advice himself.

"Doc, I'm a peaceable man, and there's not going to be any next time if I have anything to say about it."

While Shad was seeing the doctor, Abe escorted Anne to the Judge's vacant town house. There he supplied her with some of Lark's clothes and a bar of lavender-scented soap.

When Shad left the doctor's office, properly patched and bandaged, he found his old friend waiting outside.

"She all right?" he asked.

"Oh, yes," Abe assured him. "She's getting herself cleaned up. I told her that we'd be staying right across the way at my place. She knows she needs to have a talk with Martin Brent in the morning. I told her that he was the one who'd be reading the Judge's will."

"Guess I could use a little cleaning up myself," said Shad. "And you'd better find a bar of soap too, before Lark gets wind of you."

Abe chuckled. "Could be you're right about that."

That night Shad bedded down in Abe's adobe house. For the first time in a long time he had a sense of rightness about things. Actually, it was the first time since he'd discovered the Judge's body.

The next morning, the two of them escorted a rested, well-dressed young woman to the lawyer's office. There she learned from Martin Brent that she was an heiress. Abe was officially told that he'd inherited the Judge's town property, and Shad was now one hundred per cent owner of the M Bar W.

The story of Anne's kidnapping and rescue had spread like wildfire all over Trinidad. Those who'd been suspicious suddenly forgot their hostility. One even tried to apologize as they were leaving the lawyer's office.

Anne's last act before leaving town for her ranch was to wire the Bolins in Denver that she was safe and well and to invite them for a visit. Abe had a buggy ready for her. He drove while Shad rode beside them on McBeth.

"I know you'll like my wife, Lark," said Abe. "She's been awful worried about your safety. She'll be right pleased to finally meet you."

Anne smiled at him. "I'm eager to meet her as well.

Papa told me about all of you. You were like his family. I only wish I could have met you sooner."

Shad wished so too. In his opinion the Judge had made a mistake in keeping his daughter hidden. He should have brought her to Trinidad long ago and not cared what people thought or said. What was so wonderful about being a senator, anyway?

But a wrong had finally been righted, it appeared, and Anne Madison was going home at last.